THE TASTE OF TEMPTATION

THE TASTE OF TEMPTATION

Maria Lyonesse

LIBRIS

www.xratedbooks.co.uk

An *X Libris* Book

First published in Great Britain as a paperback original in 2004
by X Libris

A CIP catalogue record for this book
is available from the British Library.

ISBN 0 7515 3547 8

Typeset in Palatino by
Derek Doyle & Associates, Liverpool
Printed and bound in Great Britain by
Clays Ltd, St Ives plc

X Libris
An imprint of
Time Warner Books UK
Brettenham House
Lancaster Place
London WC2E 7EN

CHAPTER

1

Lia stretched and rolled over in bed. Then she stretched again. What a luxury to have this much space! The sheer size of Denny's double bed was as delicious as what they got up to in it.

Still grinning she rolled back and looked at the sleeping Denny. In unguarded moments like these she could almost get sentimental. Asleep, he looked so much younger. Not that she really knew his age. Mid-thirties she guessed but he'd been cagey. She didn't know details like his date of birth or why his ex-wife had left him. But she knew the most important thing: however unconventional their relationship, Denny was someone she could rely on.

One of his arms was thrown out over the duvet. Lia touched it gently. Solid muscle. Just like his shoulders and the warm and welcoming pecs that were hidden under the duvet now but whose texture she knew so well. Denny didn't work out. He didn't need to. Shifting crates and barrels of real ale around all day meant the landlord of the Boatman's Rest wasn't the sort of man who'd go to seed.

Lia moved upwards and began to stroke his hair. Soft, very curly hair that always looked an unruly mass even though he kept it short. It was so good to feel against her cheek, her lips, her breasts.

'Hey, sleepy,' she whispered. 'I feel insulted. You haven't seen me for a whole month. And you'd rather be catching up on zeds than making up for lost time?'

Denny opened his eyes and smiled back. 'Your fault, you hussy. You wore me out last night.'

'If it's all too much for you, I'll—'

Denny snaked his arms round and caught her fast under the duvet. Lia wriggled. But his arms were clamped round her waist. Even in a play-fight she had no chance.

'You're going nowhere,' he chuckled.

He rolled on top of her, pinning her in the good old missionary position. He had an early-morning hard-on already. She could feel it twanging backwards and forwards between her thighs. But she knew he was going to keep her waiting for it.

'Too horny for your own good, you are.' He smiled again. 'Anyone would think you'd been living like a nun since I last saw you . . . Okay, I know, none of my business what you get up to when you're out and about on that barge. Though living with two dykes in close confinement, I can begin to guess.'

He writhed his body against hers. The luxuriant hair on his well-muscled chest tickled her breasts. Lia moaned and squirmed; the light, teasing touch made her impatient for more. But, fed up with

2

people pigeonholing her friends, she wasn't going to let a remark like that go unchallenged.

'Only Jules is a lesbian. You know that. Trudi just likes to keep her options open.'

'Oh yeah? And right now, cooped up on the *Lady Jayne* at the bottom of my beer garden, what d'you reckon they're doing?'

'Sleeping? It is . . .' she craned her neck to see Denny's bedside clock, 'only quarter to seven.'

'Then more fool them for wasting time. There's something about these early summer mornings when it's already light . . . Must be the sap rising.'

The tip of his cock nudged her pussy again and they both giggled at the double entendre. Lia was getting impatient. She wanted him now – never mind any foreplay. But Denny seemed to have gone off on his own fantasy and was enjoying it.

'You're wrong, I'll bet,' he continued. 'I reckon those two girls are tucked up in one of those narrow bunks getting on with something like this . . .'

He eased himself down her body a little and began to kiss her breasts. Lia moaned at the pleasure of it. She even liked the scratchiness of his stubble against her soft skin as he trailed his nose and lips around and around her nipple. She loved the roughness. That was something Jules missed out on.

'Do they ever ask you to join in?' Denny murmured as he nuzzled his way down her cleavage. 'Trudi and Jules, I mean. I can't imagine you've all been living and working together for over a year and the idea's never occurred to anyone. You know, some night when it's just the three of you and maybe you've had a little too much to drink . . .'

3

'Behave. You know what I like.'

'Aren't you ever curious?' He was kissing his way further down her body now. He'd mouthed around her sensitive navel and was about to disappear beneath the duvet. Lia shivered in anticipation of Denny's enthusiastic but skilful oral sex. On the other hand she ached to be filled with his meaty cock again. It was a sweet dilemma.

He paused, though, and looked up. 'Because if you're ever tempted, could I watch? That Trudi's really something. Legs that go on for ever and fantastic tits. And she knows it.'

Lia playfully cuffed him round the head. 'Trying to make me jealous?'

Denny hauled himself up on her body again. 'I'd rather make you squeal.'

With that he penetrated her in one confident movement. Lia gasped. She was juicy and ready for him, even with minimal foreplay. And it was so good to feel his cock stretching and satisfying her again. Such a simple pleasure, his body moving and thrusting within hers. But it was enough. She was so sensitive, so horny for him. She simply relaxed, swept her hands up and over his broad, strong back and enjoyed the stirring friction as he rode her.

The warm morning and Denny's exertions meant his scent soon flooded their space. It was a very masculine scent – one which still had echoes of sex from the night before. Lia drew it deep into her lungs. She could become addicted.

She was close now. She raised her hips more to meet his thrusts. She was coming. It felt so extra special to come and feel herself spasm and pulse against a wildly thrusting cock.

Denny stepped up a gear. When he knew she'd been satisfied he went all out for his own climax and she felt the swelling, bursting feeling inside her as he did. And it was more than just his cock bucking or the extra pressure within her as he came. It was as if the sheer physical joy of his orgasm passed from his cock to her super-sensitive quim.

He collapsed down on her chest, kissing her moist, salty breasts. 'And I could do that all over again,' he breathed. 'You might not have been behaving yourself over the past month but I assure you I have. Just let me think about your delightful colleagues rubbing each other up the right way for a few moments and I'll be all ready to go.'

She dug him in the ribs. 'While you're indulging your predictable male fantasies, has there been any post for us?'

Denny rolled aside and scratched his curly head. 'Yeah. Somewhere here.' He rooted in his bedside cabinet. 'Don't know why you still need to use me as a 'care of' address. What about that whiz kid computer hacker in town who does all your web site stuff?'

A cynical edge crept into his voice as he said this and it wasn't lost on her. She knew perfectly well what Denny thought of Jonathan Harper. And why.

'He's legit these days. Has his own business. He never hacks. Well, hardly. And anyway, Jonathan doesn't believe in paper. He loses it. And if you're my postman, it means I have to make an excuse to come and see you.' She paused and kissed the back of his neck, working her way slowly round to his throat as he eased himself over and handed her several weeks' accumulated mail. 'Ah, thanks.'

Lia took the wad of envelopes and began to rifle through them. Denny snuggled up behind and nestled his still-damp cock into the cleft of her arse. As he rubbed it against her he really did seem intent on fulfilling his promise.

It was tempting. Denny was Mr Reliable and one thing she could certainly rely on him for was a horny erection that could deliver the goods. Lia snaked her arse against him. Just let him stew for a little longer, she thought; just while I check for anything important.

'Can I have some fun,' he whispered in her ear, 'while you're checking that stuff?'

He reached round and cupped her breasts in his hands. As he fondled, she could feel his cock stiffen even more against her behind.

'I'm sure your breasts are firmer than when I first met you,' he continued. 'Must be all that exercise – winding up lock gates and hauling on the ropes and stuff. Does your pec muscles good. Your cleavage is certainly more pronounced these days.'

He was running his fingers up and down it. Lia sighed. It was getting really, really hard to concentrate on the post. Still . . . One for Trudi – South African postmark: must be her folks. A couple of music magazines for Jules. The usual bumph that came with running a catering business. The VAT return – yeuch. Jules was the figures expert: she could deal with that. Ah, one addressed to them all from Auntie Faye. Bless her, Lia thought. Auntie Faye came from a more genteel age and didn't believe in texts or e-mails. Or even typewriters, from the look of the handwriting on the envelope. She slipped it open.

Ten seconds later, Lia was flying out of the bed, grabbing her clothes and leaving Denny priapic, empty handed and thoroughly confused.

In the long galley kitchen of the *Lady Jayne*, the three of them squashed round the table in silence, passing Faye's letter backwards and forwards and hoping, each time, it would say something different.

My dear girls,

Indulge a rather old-fashioned godmother but I wanted to tell you this more personally than a solicitor's letter. I'm afraid my stocks and shares have been performing poorly lately and my accountant has persuaded me to realise the profit on some of my less vital assets. Accordingly, I have arranged to sell the *Lady Jayne* to a Mr Peter Holme-Lacy. He seems a gentleman, and I'm sure you girls will get along fine with him. Indeed, it might be a perfect business opportunity as he has far more useful contacts in the hospitality sector than I do. Of course, he might be looking over your shoulders a little more than a not very 'with it' old lady but I wouldn't have sold him the boat if I didn't think you couldn't come to some amicable working relationship. I expect he will be in touch himself very soon.

Always affectionately,
Faye Montgomery

Lia felt the other two glaring at her. After all, Faye was *her* godmother – Trudi and Jules barely knew her. She felt responsible.

'Guys, I didn't know this was happening,

7

honest! I'm as pissed off as you.'

Trudi snorted. But she seemed to believe Lia's innocence. 'Where does this leave us? Legally, I mean.'

'He can't touch the business. That's ours. Straight and Narrow Catering is us – the three of us. How does it go on the web site? Our "unique blend of multicultural expertise". But the *Lady Jayne* itself belongs to Auntie Faye – or did. She paid for it to be fitted out as a floating kitchen. And we never did make enough profit in the first year to start paying her off. We're going to have to live with this. You never know, Auntie Faye might be right. Even I've heard of Peter Holme-Lacey. He's some big shot in the conference organising game. There was a thing about him last month in those trade magazines we keep getting. What with all his other business interests he might be a hands-off, decent sort of guy.'

Trudi's lip curled. She craned over and looked out of the porthole. 'Oh yeah and there's a flying bacon butty – no offence, Jules – just gone past the window.'

Just then Lia's mobile trilled from one of the cabins. Jules leaped up to get it.

'You've got a text. It's from *him*! He gets up early in the mornings . . .' She walked back slowly to the galley, reading it aloud. 'Understand you at Boatman's Rest. Must meet. See you thurs.'

'That gives us three days.' Trudi tapped a perfect fingernail against her very white teeth as she thought. It was a habit of hers, Lia had noticed over the past year or so. Then something else occurred to her: living and working so close together, who else did they know as well as they knew each other? And it worked. Whatever happened, they had to find a way to carry this on – unspoilt. 'Question:' Trudi continued, 'how does he know we're here?'

'Our itinerary is up on the web site,' Lia answered.

'Exactly. So we've got to change what the web site says. Throw him off the scent. Buy us a bit of time to work out how we're going to react to this.'

'You're suggesting we put duff information up on the web site? Deliberately sabotage our biggest marketing tool?'

'Oh, but is it, Li? What really draws the punters? Not the web site. We turn up at someone's pub, the landlord puts a board up outside like Denny does, saying something like "The Girls Are Back In Town!" and the regulars flood in. Listen, here's my plan. I go see Jonathan – lucky we were so near Stratford when this happened and Jonathan's only five miles away – get the details changed on-line and then text Peter Holme-Whatsit back and tell him to meet us somewhere else altogether. But what I tell him will agree with the web site by then.'

'I'll go and see Jonathan.'

'No.'

'Don't you trust me?' The words almost stuck in Lia's throat. Trust had never been an issue before. They'd all just been having fun. Three girls fresh out of catering college and an indulgent old godmother who'd bought them a barge and fitted it out because she wanted to keep her protégée on 'the straight and narrow' as she put it, rather than lose her to some vice hotspot like London. Of course there had been squabbles – like which sauce went best with oyster mushrooms or who to fob off in what order when the bills came in – but nothing had ever seemed this serious before.

'Of course I trust you.' Trudi laid her hand on Lia's shoulder and rubbed it up and down her arm a little. 'But whatever Denny did to you last night, it must have been good. Knocked your brains out, clearly. Because we're up on the board outside as doing crêpes this lunchtime and that, sweetie, is your area of expertise. Not to mention one of the best sellers in this pub. So you and Jules get things on the go for lunch and I'll drag young Jonathan out of bed.'

Lia scowled. Why did Trudi have to use that turn of phrase about Jonathan? Just when everything seemed to be calming down again.

'Share nicely, children,' Jules chuckled as she got up to start clearing their breakfast things away, 'I'm sure there's enough of Jonathan for both of you.'

Thanks, Jules, Lia thought, thanks a bunch. It never used to bother me whether Trudi had the occasional fling with him or not. Why does it now?

Trudi eased out from behind the table. She was wearing very tight denim shorts this morning. They bared the lower curves of her incredibly pert bottom. And Lia had to agree with Denny – she did have amazing legs. A stab of something hit her and she wasn't sure if it was jealousy or curiosity.

As Trudi climbed up out of the hatch, Jules slapped her behind in a way that was friendly yet proprietary at the same time. It made Lia feel uneasy. Of course she'd always known the other two slept together in a no-ties sort of way. It had never made her feel the odd one out before. Up on deck she heard the two of them talking.

'Denny's got a bike I can borrow to get into town, hasn't he?'

'If you ask nicely,' Jules replied. 'But not too nicely. I think you've already stepped on the boss's toes once too often this morning.'

The boss? Just because her godmother had put up the money in the first place. In the fifteen months they'd been working together the other two had never referred to her like that before. They'd been equal partners – that had been understood. Lia rested her head in her hands and moaned. All this and it wasn't even half past nine yet. Why couldn't she have just left the post and had another enjoyable hour in bed with Denny?

And as if they needed any more setbacks that day, at quarter past ten – when Jules was slicing courgettes and tomatoes, and Lia was carefully mixing the light, fine batter for the galletes – there was a sharp rap on the hatch. A man stuck his head inside.

'Paul Gillespie, Environmental Health Department, South Warwickshire District Council.' He flashed a laminated photocard at them. 'You were expecting me?'

Lia and Jules shrugged at each other. This must have been something Trudi had set up.

'Is Ms Van der Plaas here?' he continued – and seemed relieved she wasn't. Lia thought she knew why and chuckled. Trudi made a point of trying to seduce environmental health inspectors. She seemed to see it as a challenge. Whenever they turned up – poking around, taking swabs off their preparation surfaces and samples out of their fridge – she'd be there, lounging against the next

surface and crossing and uncrossing her outrageously long legs. Or leaning over to explain a
point, making sure her statuesque breasts slid out
of her tiny little top to their best advantage. Or
reaching up to get something from a high shelf so
her top rode up and the fascinating jewel in her
pierced navel twinkled and drew attention to itself.

Lia felt sorry for the men. Trudi must be hard to
resist. Her striking tallness came from the Dutch
side of her family. Her strong, compelling features,
mass of dark hair and sweet café au lait skin were
the result of an affair her headstrong grandmother
had, which at the time in South Africa would have
been truly unthinkable, and Trudi herself still
romanticised about it. But the inspectors did resist.
There must have been something in the health and
safety regulations about it.

This one spent an hour failing to find anything
wrong with their hygiene arrangements. He left
looking disappointed, as if three young women
doing something as off-the-wall as running a catering business from a canal barge must be doing
something wrong. Almost as soon as he'd strode off
across Denny's beer garden, Trudi came cycling
down the track beside the pub, her long legs tensing and relaxing as she pushed the pedals.

Damn it, I am *not* curious, Lia thought. Things
are just a little bit mad today.

Trudi sprang aboard and winked at Jules. At
Jules, Lia noticed. Not at both of them. 'A result,'
she declared, but didn't volunteer anything more.

Lunchtime customers were beginning to mill
into the beer garden and the girls had some time to
make up. The chaos and Lia's ever-popular
French-style galettes helped take everyone's minds

off things for a while. Lia loved being busy. And being busy doing something she knew she was good at. She was genuinely proud of her skill at cooking. The nutty buckwheat batter needed constant watching if it wasn't to burn. It was a skill – one she'd first seen practised in the little Parisian street cafés when her mother had taken her back there for long holidays as a child.

As the afternoon wore on, customers came back for sweet crêpes rather than savoury, and Lia opened bottles of maple syrup, dark chocolate sauce and the genuine *marron* purée her aunt in Poitiers had to send over; you couldn't get the proper stuff here. Some of the crêpes were over-filled and oozed as she folded them. Once she licked the spare purée straight off her finger, knowing full well environmental health would have a fit. The sweet, intense flavour paralysed her jaw for a moment. Ah, simple pleasures. It put her in a better mood.

But things still weren't right. There was an atmosphere even while the girls cleared away the lunch things and Trudi began chopping her spicy, exotic ingredients for the evening shift.

We're watching our own backs, Lia thought. This isn't the shared, inclusive thing it used to be. And I'm no better than them. Because as soon as Denny had called time and the last of the evening customers drifted away, she announced, 'I'm going out,' and left the other two to clear up.

'Out where – at this time of night?' Jules demanded.

'Just out. I need to get my head together.'

She could tell from their faces they didn't believe her and she didn't blame them.

*

Jonathan was a night owl. Always had been. When Lia slammed the taxi door behind her in the centre of Stratford-upon-Avon it was gone midnight but when she looked all the way up to his top-floor flat the lights were still on. He worked to a different timetable from everyone else, which was why Trudi's quip about 'dragging him out of bed' had been true – but unsettling. As Lia buzzed his intercom she told herself yet again she just wanted a break – to spend some time unwinding with someone whose livelihood wasn't on the line right now – rather than to check what Trudi might have done when she 'dragged him out of bed' that morning.

'Hello, stranger.' Jonathan's soft voice came over the intercom. 'Wondered when you'd turn up. Come on in.'

In her high-heeled sandals it took Lia a few minutes to climb to the top floor of that tall, Gothic, Victorian building. The whole thing belonged to some property developer uncle of Jonathan's, and he kept an eye on things in return for a cool place to live and being left largely in peace. When Lia reached the front door of his flat she found it was ajar. She pushed it open and went in. Jonathan was at the computer, about to shut down. He didn't turn. She stroked the back of his head. His hair was soft, dark, loose down to his shoulders with a little curl at the end and shot through with streaks of purple highlights.

'Didn't interrupt any work, I hope?' she murmured.

'You're always more interesting than work.'

He tipped his head back to look up at her. He had an angular face, not good looking in a conventional sense, but Lia had always felt there was something about Jonathan. Something ambiguous. Something unpredictable. It made for that indefinable thing lovers call 'chemistry'.

'Right now you look like you need a drink,' he continued.

'Wait. Just a minute. Don't shut that thing off. Show me what you've done to my web site first.'

Did I say 'my' web site? she wondered as Jonathan logged back on to the Internet. They're right. I am getting possessive. Acting like the boss.

He stood up and made way for her on the chair. As she waited for the little blue line to creep infuriatingly slowly across its window, Jonathan began massaging her shoulders.

She closed her eyes and let him undo the knotted muscles with his fine, practised hands. Jonathan was so good at this. Him and Denny – they were utterly different. Denny was an uncomplicated dose of sheer old-fashioned masculinity. Jonathan was something . . . less easy to define. Lia sighed and let his sensitive hands turn her body to compliant running water.

But did you do this for Trudi? she wondered. Did you offer to rub her feet after she'd cycled over here, and then moved on up those amazon, fantastic legs?

Damn. Business first. She opened her eyes and forced herself to concentrate on the computer screen.

'It's good,' she admitted. 'Very convincing. Thanks.'

'Trudi did most of it. She's got more initiative than you give her credit for.'

'Okay. I consider myself duly taken down a peg or two. But don't stop – oh, yes, lower . . .'

'Your problem,' he whispered in her ear as he bent

lower and worked his finger magic further down her spine, 'is that you girls have never been good at long-term planning. You've been too busy enjoying yourselves doing what you're good at. And you are good. But you're going to have to learn fast.'

'Tell me in the morning.' She began logging off the computer. 'Right now I need to forget.'

'You want that drink?'

'A drink would be a start.'

'Before I forget, I printed out the 'real' web site stuff before we changed it. Just so you don't forget where you're supposed to be.'

'Hard copy? Jonathan, I'm touched. Better put it in my bag before you work your disappearing magic on it.'

He poured them both peach schnapps and they flopped down on one of his oversized sofas, which were covered with ethnic throws. Jonathan's flat was a combination of the gleaming metal of his computers, servers and state-of-the-art monitors, and spice-coloured African fabrics. But no paper. He really didn't believe in it.

'So Trudi filled you in on this Peter Holme-Whatsit business,' she stated as she swirled the viscous schnapps in her glass. She hated giving him his proper name. If she could make a joke of it maybe she didn't need to take him so seriously.

'Yeah. Bit of a shock. But you will pull through it – the three of you. You always have. You're just going to need to adapt.'

'I don't know. Something about this is different. I'm scared it's going to split us up.'

Jonathan put down his glass and reached over to massage her shoulders again. 'Hey, this is really getting to you. You've got knots all the way down here. I felt them before. Let me . . . Hey, don't go to sleep on me! I didn't plan on relaxing you that much.'

He eased his slim body closer and began kissing the side of her neck. Lia heard a tiny sound coming from her own throat – halfway between a ticklish giggle and moan of desire. Jonathan's lips were just as skilful as his fingers. There was a coolness about them that was more erotic than she would have expected. A soft clinginess, too, as they travelled up and down the curve of her throat. Jonathan was in no hurry. It was one of the strange bonuses of his unconventional timekeeping: many times before in their off/on relationship he'd happily let foreplay last till three o'clock in the morning.

But Lia was in a hurry. At least this time. She wanted to forget herself for a while, and kisses and sweet, peachy alcohol alone weren't enough for that.

'Let's go next door, Jonathan. We can get more comfortable.'

He stood up and led her by the hand into his bedroom. A twist on the dimmer switch gave the room a soft, sensuous glow. He slept on a futon – low and wide. They sank down together on to it. His purple-shot, dark hair fell forwards on to her face like thousands of whispering, sensual kisses.

She glided her hands down over his body. Jonathan was wearing a silky shirt and soft, Indian-style trousers. She loved the feel of them. She could easily become a texture junkie. The different fabrics slipped and slid over his body and the warmth from beneath seeped through against her palms. She cradled and fondled his buttocks. There was so little resistance surely he must be wearing silk boxers beneath? Jonathan had a thing

17

about silk next to his skin. Lia walked her hands round and cupped his groin. Everything there, too, was expanding in an unfettered way.

'If I didn't know better,' she whispered, 'I could believe you've been saving this for me.'

'Believe it.' He kissed her.

'And Trudi?'

He chuckled. 'Trudi is sex on legs.' He began kissing up along the bridge of her nose and over her eyelids, closing them and making her surrender. 'And you know damn well what I think of her legs. But no – not this time.'

'Liar. She had that smirk on her face when she got back to the boat.' Lia was having difficulty concentrating as Jonathan kissed the margins of her hair and twirled his long, mobile tongue into her ear. It made her shiver. 'The one she has when she's just been laid.'

'Well, it wasn't me.' He was moving down her body now, kissing her throat and nudging down the neckline of her tight summer top. 'But I'll tell you a funny story if you like.'

'Will it turn me on?' Lia couldn't decide whether she wanted to be distracted from Jonathan's leisurely, indulgent foreplay or whether she wanted to know the truth.

'Maybe.' He slid his body even further down the bed and tried a new angle to get into her clothes. He eased up her clingy top and began kissing her belly, circling her navel with his probing tongue and making her squirm with pleasure again. 'We were just finishing up on the web site stuff,' he said between kisses, 'when one of Uncle Neil's new tenants from downstairs knocked on the door for something. Attractive woman. Petite. Red haired. I never realised she was a traffic warden until I saw her in the uniform today. But she and Trudi just took one look at each other and, well . . . if she was smirking when she got back to the boat it was the uniform that did it, not me.'

Lia began giggling. Partly in relief, partly at the bizarreness of the situation. She'd never guessed Trudi had a uniform fetish.

'Keep still, woman,' Jonathan growled. 'How am I supposed to create my oral masterpiece on a jiggling canvas?'

Lia held her breath and tried to keep still. The sensations of Jonathan's weaving tongue on her sensitive flesh really were so mind-blowingly sexy. There was no one else who knew how to play her quite so well. Here they were – he fully clothed and she near as, damn it, but already she couldn't believe how aroused she was. Too aroused to wait much longer.

'What do you fancy?' she whispered.

'Silk games?'

Lia smiled. They'd been casual lovers long enough to have their little shorthands and codes.

She rolled him over and took control. She unbuttoned his soft, flowing shirt and kissed his chest beneath. Yes, she was desperate for sex but not so desperate she couldn't linger here a moment, chasing her nose through Jonathan's fine sprinkling of chest hair, playing dot-to-dot on his birthmarks with her tongue, drinking in his unique scent.

Then she eased his loose trousers and boxer shorts over his narrow, bony hips. His erection sprang free into her face. It was paler, slimmer, but longer than Denny's bullish cock. Right at this moment, though, she felt she loved it more than any other possibility.

19

There was something about Jonathan's cock that always touched the perfect spot inside her.

Once Jonathan was naked she rolled over and delved in the tasteful little wicker basket beside the bed. Inside was a tangled mass of long, narrow silk scarves in a jumble of vivid, jewel-like colours. She pulled four out of the mass and began to tie his wrists and ankles to heavy steel rings bolted to each corner of the futon. They'd never been included in the original IKEA flat pack.

Jonathan didn't resist. He closed his eyes, sighed and moaned as he felt the silk clasp his limbs and secure him down. When he was well trussed, Lia eased a fifth cerise silk scarf from the tangle and draped it across his swollen cock just to give him something to be going on with.

She stood at the foot of the bed – in his full view but unattainable. She stripped off her clothes. Yes, she was impatient, but she wanted to tease. She pulled her tight vest top up over her head. In the hot summer night she hadn't been wearing a bra underneath and her firm breasts bobbed free. Jonathan rolled his hips and writhed a little in his bonds as her clothes came off. But she'd tied him up tight – the way he liked it.

Her flimsy skirt whispered to the floor. She peeled off her panties. But she left her high-heeled sandals on. Then she prowled over Jonathan on the bed.

She lifted the cerise silk scarf she'd left draped over his cock. She snapped a length of it tight between her hands and then began gliding it backwards and forwards against the underside of his shaft.

It made a strange rustling sound as she did so. Under the pressure, his erection rolled a little from side to side. The stretched, pink silk was virtually see-through, and the sight of his cock rolling and darkening beneath her was sexual in a very visual, graphic way. Jonathan's mounting excitement began weeping from that single eye and soaking into the scarf. Lia judged the time was right.

She snatched up the silk scarf again and pressed it against his face, letting him drink in the scent of his own arousal. She brought her hips level with his and then impaled her moist sex on his erection.

As always, Jonathan's long, slim cock excited her as it travelled deep into her body. For a while she rode him in a slow, teasing action, letting her hips grind a figure of eight. His cock was sparking just the right spot. A diffuse pleasure was filling her clitoris as she pressed her mons against his bony pubis. He strained against his bonds, impatient at the last and trying to thrust more wildly into her body. But he was restricted. She controlled the pace.

Lia altered her position, leaned forwards and rubbed her breasts against his crinkly chest hair as she rode him. She was so close herself now. That little extra nipple stimulation was bringing her closer all the time. She came only seconds before he did, the feeling of his warm explosion in her sex making her own orgasm all the more fulfilling.

'Can I stay?' she whispered as she relaxed down beside him and began undoing the knots she'd tightened. With Jonathan it always felt warm and loving afterwards even though they knew they had no hold over each other.

He nodded. While she knew it wouldn't solve anything, Lia was grateful for the breathing space. And for a bed that wouldn't rock if a boat went by.

CHAPTER

2

It had seemed a good idea – sneaking back by taxi at seven o'clock in the morning. Trudi and Jules would still be asleep. But then, Lia thought, why all this sneaking around anyway? She could just as well have been in Denny's bed, as she had been the previous night.

She was wrong. Trudi and Jules were up already, drinking strong espresso coffee and finishing up the remains of last night's sweet waffles for breakfast.

'So where precisely was "out"?' Trudi asked coolly.

'Jonathan's.'

'Were you checking up on me?'

'Of course not. Just needed to remind myself what a cute arse he's got.'

'Lia Berrier, you are a useless liar. Were you checking up on me?'

'Okay.'

'In every sense?'

'Yes.'

'And?'

'You did a good job. I'm sorry.' She sighed. 'And I'm sorry if I've been snappy these past twenty-four hours. We've all got our own ways of dealing with this mess.'

'And that's fine, but not if those ways irritate the hell out of the other members of the crew,' Trudi said. 'There are three people on this boat. Remember that. We can get through this together but only if we get through it *together*. Agreed?'

Lia nodded. 'Okay. No secrets. Even little ones. And that Jonathan is a randy, kinky bastard, as I'm sure you know, Trudi. I got about four hours' sleep last night. So you guys better not have finished that coffee.'

Jules grinned as she passed over the pot. 'Best friends in the whole wide world and all that cheesy stuff. Remember, like Trudi says, we need each other if we're going to pull through this. Group hug?'

They chuckled as they hugged and the awkward atmosphere of the previous day seemed to evaporate. For a moment. Then there was a loud rap on the hatch and they all froze in each other's arms.

Jules went to look. It was Mike, Denny's assistant barman.

'Get the engine started and get the hell out of here,' he said, breathlessly. 'I'll give you a hand to cast off. No time to explain but your Holme-Lacey geezer is here. Denny's keeping him talking. Go down the river about two hundred yards – round the bend and the trees will cover you. Get moving!'

There wasn't even any time to panic. They pushed off from the bank and chugged down the river at the barge's agonising top speed of four miles an hour. Lia, steering, kept looking back over her shoulder. Her stomach was clenched tight: at any moment an expensive-suited man might come strolling down over the dew-dusted lawns of Denny's beer garden. But no one came. She breathed a silent thank you. You didn't run a pub for years and years without developing the gift of the gab, and Denny had it better than most. She'd underestimated him.

There was a spot down-river where massive, cave-like weeping willows had overgrown the path. They moored up there – with difficulty but the cover made it worthwhile. Lia sat on deck, clutching her mobile phone and waiting for the text to come from Denny telling them the coast was clear. Trudi and Jules were crouching half under the table in the galley. Why were they doing that? If they weren't hidden enough by the distance from the pub and the trailing willows then skulking like naughty schoolgirls wasn't going to be much help.

But Trudi seemed to be getting off on this cloak-and-dagger stuff. Lia felt a stab of annoyance. This was childish. Here they were trying to outwit a genuine, grown up threat, and Trudi and Jules were giggling under the table groping each other like teenagers. Perhaps they were carrying on something she'd interrupted with her breakfast-time entrance? Lia felt shut out of the loop again.

Out of the loop, she thought. That never used to happen – not even when I knew full well Jules and Trudi were sleeping together. The fact they had something going I wasn't party to never used to bother me. It didn't make a difference to our friendship. Like that time when we'd all had a bit

24

to drink, and Trudi put her arms round me tight and said, 'Just 'cause I'm sleeping with Jules and not you, doesn't mean you're not my very best mate.' Denny got it so wrong. Men do. When we had a few drinks inside us we didn't get horny – we got sentimental.

Heavy footfalls crunched along the path in a jogging rhythm. Lia jumped and looked round. It was okay. It was Denny.

'Thought I'd come myself and give you a hand turning this baby round.' He breathed heavily and rested against the side of the *Lady Jayne* for a moment. 'You're in the clear. Holme-Lacey's gone.'

'What the hell was he doing coming after us at this time in the morning?' Jules popped her head out of the hatch. Lia could see Trudi below in the galley looking almost piqued at the interruption.

'On his way to the airport – so he said. He's got an emergency business meeting in Brussels so he had to change his plans for seeing you. He dropped in on his way to Birmingham International on the offchance. And I had to think on the spot, which isn't easy for a bloke like me at this hour.' He straightened up and grinned at Lia. 'The things I do for you girls.'

There was still sweat on his forehead from his sudden dash down the towpath. Lia felt a stab of tenderness for him, which took her quite off guard. And a vague sense of guilt. Denny and Jonathan – they knew about each other. Or at least they knew she wasn't exactly doing her knitting when she was away from either of them. She stamped hard on the old-fashioned feelings that had sneaked up. They weren't appropriate right now.

'So what did you tell him?' Jules insisted.

'I was quite proud of myself. Told him you'd been having some problems with your web site recently – some rival catering firm had hacked into it and put up all the wrong dates and venues, but if he wanted to look again it should be all right now. He looked at me as if he knew there was something fishy going on – and I don't just mean the menu. But he's gone. And he won't be back for the rest of the week. So you girls can come and get some cooking done.'

'You're a star.' Jules clapped him on the shoulder. 'We owe you.'

'And you'll owe me even more when we've got the *Lady Jayne* turned round. Doing a three-point turn with a barge is a bitch, but hand me that boat hook and we'll see if we can't sort it.'

It was gone midnight when Lia slid into Denny's huge, bubble-filled bath with a sigh. She was feeling beat from another hard evening over the galley's stove. And yet . . . her body had gone to a place beyond tiredness. She wouldn't sleep for a few hours yet. Especially as Denny himself was sitting at the tap end of the decadently big bathtub.

'It's bliss to have so much space,' she murmured. 'That shower on the boat is tiny. We've got to crouch to get in it. Especially Trudi.'

'Ooh, don't you get me thinking about that Trudi in the shower. Her naked, steamy body and water coursing down that incredible cleavage she's always flashing in people's faces. I'm having a very clichéd male response just imagining it.'

Lia giggled and slipped her hand under the mounds of foam. She ran her palm along her own smooth leg and then on to Denny's thicker, hairier thighs twined between them.

'Liar,' she said as she found his cock; it was still soft.

'Yeah, well that's only 'cause it's been a long day.' He leaned forwards and started kissing her. 'And I do so love winding you up.'

Lia giggled again, her lips clamped to his. It was true, though. There was something edgy about imagining Denny fantasising about the tall, assertive, voluptuous Trudi. That he was attracted to her, she didn't doubt. Most men were. Would he ever overstep the mark and make a pass at her? Trudi was hardly one to refuse. The little frisson of jealousy added a pinch of spice.

I'm greedy, she thought, even as Denny's kisses became greedier. I want two lovers. But the thought of either of them with other women pushes my insecurity buttons.

'It's a very big bath,' he murmured, breaking off from their deep-tongued kiss.

Lia frowned, confused for a moment at this direction. Yes, it was a big bath, in a most un-Denny-like, indulgent bathroom en suite to his bedroom above the seventeenth-century pub. Right now it was surrounded by candles placed on shelves which seemed to be there just for the purpose. Denny was practical in a down-to-earth, blokey sort of way. She could only assume this was his ex-wife's taste, and another little jealous frisson shivered its way through her lower belly.

'Big enough,' he continued, in between kissing his way down her neck, 'for three, perhaps? Even when the third is a big girl like Trudi. Go on. The phone's in the next room. Give her a quick ring on

27

the mobile. Ask her if she fancies coming to join us if the shower on board is so cramped.'

Confusing thoughts began to party in Lia's head. Of course she'd seen Trudi naked. You don't share a flat with someone for three years at catering college and then an even smaller space on a barge for more than a year and stay coy – especially with Trudi's non-Anglo-Saxon attitudes. But that had been a functional, off-hand nakedness. What Denny was suggesting was decidedly sexual.

'I never know when you're being serious. And, anyway, she wouldn't thank me for ringing. She's probably got the mobile turned off and is snuggled up in a bunk with Jules right now.'

'You don't half say the right things to get a bloke turned on. The thought of that strapping, dusky wench with her kinky body piercing and that cute little tomboy doing their tongue and groove stuff . . . And all going to waste with nobody watching . . .'

She slipped her hand down again under the foam that was still rich and creamy. Denny's cock was beginning to meat up with interest. But he still wasn't properly erect.

'Well, well. It must have been a long day,' she whispered. 'Lie back and think of England, eh?'

Denny grinned and lay back full length in the bath. She picked up one of his long, narrow feet and wiped off the foam meticulously. Then she put his middle toe to her lips and began to tongue it slowly. Denny had curiously sexy feet. She loved to watch him padding round his flat dressed only in his work-faded jeans with his bare, hairy chest and bare feet showing. He had long toes and the middle one protruded almost a centimetre past the big one. They were lovely toes to suck. And it had a dramatic effect on him.

Her only regret right now was that she couldn't see it in action. Many times she'd done this to him while they lay on his big double bed. It was something he'd asked her to do fairly early on in their relationship. Whether it was a little trick of his ex-wife's, she'd never wanted to know, but sucking Denny's middle toe was like dialling a hot line direct to his cock.

She loved to watch it happening. She loved to see Denny lie back naked on the bed and watch his cock swell, roll and flip up, standing tall towards his belly button as if by remote control. And when she'd sucked his toes first, his erection always seemed to be particularly strong and long lasting.

Right now, though, his cock was hidden beneath an over-extravagant mass of bubbles. They should never, Lia thought as she ran her tongue up and down the underside of his toe and teased the little webbed space between, have been so mad as to empty half the bottle in. She kept watch carefully. If something happened she didn't want to miss it.

Sure enough there was a disturbance under the bubbles – a flick in the foam as if a small animal had breached the surface and dived down again. And a definite hint of pink under the mass of creamy white froth.

Denny grinned and hauled himself up to a sitting position. 'One of these days I'm going to get you to do that for ages to see if it's enough to bring me off. But right now I haven't got the patience.'

Lia sat up to meet him and grinned back. 'You never have.'

He took two handfuls of foam and began to soap her breasts with them. She was amazed how rich the lather had stayed. It felt almost like body lotion being rubbed into her skin. The gliding sensuality of it made Denny's touch so much more intense, so different from just skin on bare skin. He tried to fondle her breasts but the whipped-up lather made them slippery and hard to grasp. It was frustrating for him, but Lia found the way his hands skated across her skin and just missed squeezing her nipples was turning her on.

Denny knelt up fully. His erection, dripping warm water, reared above her. It was so virile. Un-PC though it was, she loved the thought of being dominated by it. And right now, level with her face, it did seem very dominant. Her automatic reaction was to part her lips and take him in, dripping with foam or not. But Denny cupped her face in his hands and held her back.

'You give a great blow job, kid, but right now I fancy something else and you've got me too close to risk any more of your mouth magic. Kneel up, yeah? Turn round.'

She did as he asked and leaned forwards a little, taking her weight on the generous shelf at the side of the bath. As her skin was exposed to the air again she felt the pricklish tickle of foam popping and drying on her skin. Just as well it was a warm, sultry night.

Behind her, Denny was fondling and moulding her buttocks. Lia arched her back a little more, trying to shove her arse in his face. She felt his hand, covered in foam again, slip up and down her secret cleft. The creaminess still hadn't fully vanished and his touch felt at the same time very clean and very dirty. Then he reached round further and began to finger her pussy.

The only problem with sex in the bath was that the water robbed her of much of her natural lubrication. But Lia was easily turned on; Denny's expert fingering was getting her juices running again. Once he knew he had her good and moist he worked a couple of thick fingers inside her. There was something about Denny's fingers. Years of hard physical work, rolling barrels, pulling pints and hefting crates had swollen and roughened them. So different from Jonathan's more sensitive, almost feminine touch. When Denny touched her – especially touched her inside – she knew all about it.

Lia moaned. She was seriously horny now. 'You still good and hard?' she whispered.

'What do you think?'

Denny withdrew his fingers from her pussy and rubbed his erection up and down against her slippery buttocks. How she loved the feel of it. But really it had been just an excuse to make him do it. She knew damn well that after a toe-sucking treat Denny's erection never flagged until he'd come inside her.

She leaned forwards a little more, parted her wet thighs and offered him the perfect angle to penetrate her. Denny's cock slipped in, confident and lusty. She felt every inch of him rear high up inside her, satisfying her intense need to be filled. He began thrusting, slowly at first. When he was sure of his stroke he reached round and began fondling both her breasts.

They had dried in the air by now. He got a good grip and squeezed and tweaked her nipples as he thrust. She was sure his cock was growing harder and fuller inside her as he responded to this tactile stimulation. She sank forwards against the edge of the bath. It was just the perfect height.

As Denny rammed into her – more savagely now – with every thrust home her tender mons Veneris was squeezed against the unyielding enamel bath. It wasn't as direct as clitoral stimulation. It was more diffuse. But the sensations were amazing. More and more, Lia became convinced this whole bathroom had been designed for sex.

There was a mirror screwed to the tiled wall a foot or so in front of her. It had been steamed up by the bath and was becoming even more steamed up by her rapid breath. She couldn't make out herself or Denny distinctly; she could see only the heaving, flesh-coloured shapes of a big, overbearing man and a smaller woman. Occasionally Denny might rear up into a clearer patch of mirror and she could see his distinctive, curly hair, reminding her it was really Denny. Otherwise he could have been anonymous. The possibility thrilled her.

Or, more than that. She imagined she was watching a porn video. She couldn't make out her own features at all – just the vague shape of darker hair against a pale skin and the movement of her breasts. Denny could be fucking anyone. She played with those delicious, prickles of jealousy and was curious to find the fantasy aroused her further.

The bump and grind of her mons against the bath had brought her close, so close. Denny was grunting in her ear. He was a good lover. He had the sort of control a man in his thirties has learned and she knew he wouldn't come until he knew she was satisfied. Lia pressed her pelvis furiously against the side of the bath. It was wildly frustrating: in the slipperiness she couldn't find enough purchase or friction. She was hanging on the verge of orgasm but not quite there. All she could do was close her eyes and concentrate on the wonderful, pounding feelings of Denny's big stiff cock exciting the length of her quim.

And at last she was there. The fabulous free-fall sensation of being on the edge of a cliff of desire and then toppling off into space. The fall into orgasm was longer, slower than usual because her greedy, instant-gratification clitoris had been sidelined. The spasms went on and on as Denny continued thrusting for his own pleasure now as recklessly as he physically could. Still, it seemed for ever until he roared in her ear and his whole body stiffened with his orgasm. Lia grinned fiercely with several kinds of satisfaction. It was true – once she'd sucked his toes, his erection was guaranteed for a good long time.

They knelt there for a few minutes, gasping, before he withdrew. The water in the bath had grown cold now. Lia noticed it for the first time and began to shiver. Denny ran some more hot.

'I hate getting out of a cold bath,' he explained. 'And besides, we haven't given each other that all over wash yet.'

The bubbles had gone now, too. Lia poured herself a handful of shower gel and massaged it into Denny's chest while more scalding water cascaded into the bath and enveloped them in steam again. His mass of springy chest hair made the gel lather up quickly. She smiled with pleasure as she massaged the lather further up around his neck and shoulders and further down over his taut stomach.

It felt so good touching Denny's body. Not that – she glanced aside to where Denny's wristwatch had tumbled to the floor – she could expect another performance at nearly half past one in the morning with a busy day ahead of them tomorrow. But there was something close, something sensual about washing each other.

Finally Lia lay back and let him wash her smooth, slim legs. He cradled her feet, paying particular attention to the little gaps between her toes. She felt so relaxed.

'So what's he like, this Holme-Lacey bloke?' she asked sleepily. 'You never did get round to telling me.'

Denny shrugged and carried on playing with a handful of lather, moulding it into tiny peaks on her red-varnished toenails.

'Rich,' he said eventually.

'I know that! Denny, this is the guy I'm up against. I need a bit more info.'

'Okay then. Old money. Like he's got a history behind him. But a bit of an entrepreneur with it. Not one of your chinless wonders with a posh accent trading on the family heritage. And clever. You're not going to run rings round him in a hurry.'

'What's he look like?'

That wasn't meant to slip out. That was irrelevant.

'Wouldn't say he was your type – but what do I know? Average, I suppose. In a very up-market way.'

'Age?'

'Maybe forty. Difficult to tell.'

'You didn't like him, did you?'

'I don't like any bloke in a suit. They usually mean trouble.'

'We've got to know a bit more about him, Denny. Know who we're dealing with before we show our hand.'

Denny grinned mischievously. 'I've got an idea.' He leaned forwards and whispered it to her. 'Unless you're chicken, of course?'

Lia snatched her foot out of his hand and sat bolt upright, causing massive waves to slop over the side of the bath and on to the bathroom floor. 'That is the most ludicrous thing I've ever heard you say!'

CHAPTER

3

The day was so bright that the sun on any slab of concrete or bare stretch of tarmac would have blinded Lia if it wasn't for the large dark glasses she was wearing. There wasn't a cloud in the sky. The warmth felt so good on her bare skin. And there was lots of bare skin – at least on her upper body. Between them, Denny and Trudi had seen to that.

'You'll have to wear one of my tops,' Trudi had insisted first thing that morning. 'Yours are far too prim.'

'They'll never fit,' Lia had protested. Trudi not only had well-developed breasts she had broader shoulders and a big frame.

'You'd be surprised. Don't underestimate yourself. Anyway, here's one that was always a little on the tight side . . .'

Trudi produced a tiny little strappy vest top that plunged low at the front. Not only that but around the daring neckline there was a band of open lace work giving further glimpses of her breasts beneath.

'Perfect,' Trudi pronounced when Lia had put it on. 'And we'll sort you out a little fake tattoo just here.' She placed a fingertip halfway down Lia's cleavage. Lia shivered and didn't quite like to examine why. 'A little rose or something. Subtle. Just so it catches his eye. If he's staring at your tits his guard'll be down and he'll tell you anything. But first . . .' She turned and called over her shoulder into the other cabin, 'Jules, you find any yet?'

Jules came through, waving a tube of fake tan triumphantly. 'It's last year's so it's a bit sticky. And there's not much left.' She looked doubtfully at the expanse of flesh Lia was baring. 'We'll have to go easy on it. She might need to wear a long skirt – we won't have enough for her legs as well.'

'You're enjoying this, aren't you?' Lia demanded. 'Like it's a grown-up game of Barbies or something. This is serious!'

'Of course it is,' Trudi murmured as she slipped aside the straps of Lia's new, revealing top. 'Which is why we've got to get everything just right. Now let me put this stuff on. Someone else can do it much more evenly than you can on yourself. We don't want any streaks.'

Lia surrendered to Trudi's hands. She clearly knew what she was doing as she began massaging Jules's fake tan smoothly and evenly into Lia's face, neck and shoulders. In fact, Trudi had expert hands. Big, competent and powerful, but sensitive at the same time. She almost giggled as the thought hit her – Trudi was a perfect blend of Denny and Jonathan in that respect. She wondered why she'd never asked her to give her a massage. She knew Trudi massaged Jules late at night after a long day hunched over the chopping board and the stove. But then again, those massages led on to other things . . .

Curiosity was just stirring with those thoughts as Trudi's hands moved down and began smoothing the fake tan into the upper curves of Lia's breasts. Trudi had never touched her there. No woman had. She'd expected it to be a purely functional touch. But it wasn't. And she had to clamp down hard on the impure thoughts that were rising.

Jules took the tube from Trudi and began working on Lia's back. There was something special about this – something warm and inclusive about being touched by the two other women. Lia fought hard to convince herself that's all it was. Trudi and Jules had long had something private and sensual. Lia was beginning to feel they were letting her in on the secret.

'There,' Trudi said – all too soon as far as Lia was concerned. 'That should do it. We've just about got enough left to do your legs up to the knees, so wear your long, purple tie-dyed skirt and for God's sake don't keep crossing and uncrossing your legs when you talk to him. Jules, if you can get on with that I'll just go sort out the finishing touch.'

Trudi disappeared into the other cabin again and came out a few minutes later with an armful of wigs.

Jules raised an eyebrow. 'From your new friend?'

Trudi nodded. 'Just borrowed. She needs them back in good shape so no leaping in the canal or anything stupid. What'll it be? Long and blonde, curly and red, or short and dark?'

'The blonde one looks too fake,' Jules decided. 'The dark one's too short. Most men have a long hair fetish.' She raked a hand through her own punkish crop. 'Or so I've heard – not exactly my territory. Let's see what the red one looks like on.'

Lia protested. 'Fake tan and a red wig? I'll look all orange.'

'But it's totally unlike your natural colour,' Trudi insisted. 'And, given that our photos are up on the web site, the whole object of this exercise is to make you look as unlike yourself as possible, remember. Now hold still.'

When the wig was on, Lia had to admit the whole thing actually worked. It was a subtle, deep-auburn colour. It looked exotic with the tan. The wild curls made her feel vampish. She really was someone else now. She could do anything.

Trudi and Jules grinned at each other. She could tell they were pleased with their work and didn't believe for a moment they weren't still playing Barbie dolls.

'Now,' Trudi said, 'provided Denny can keep his hands off you for long enough we should be okay.' She began rifling through her make-up bag. 'Just the tattoo to go now. Not sure if I've got any roses after all . . .'

And now, late morning, Lia was wandering arm-in-arm with Denny through the riverside recreation ground that had been given over this weekend to a jazz festival. The wig was getting hot and itchy in the heat. It distracted her. And she couldn't afford to feel distracted, or irritable, or anything other than the outrageous flirt she'd set herself up to be. This had all better be worth it.

Away to her left a band were doing a sound-check on the main stage. The saxophonist was starting up. It was a low, mellow, haunting sound. Properly handled, Lia thought, no instrument is as

39

sexy as a saxophone. Cool and fluid yet sensual at the same time. She smiled. It was almost enough to help her forget her overheating scalp.

'Got him,' Denny hissed suddenly. 'Target at two o'clock, just heading towards the beer tent. See him?'

It took Lia a moment to work out who he meant. As a typical bloke, Denny couldn't possibly have described Peter Holme-Lacey in terms of what he looked like or what he was wearing. If it had been down to Lia, she would have said something along the lines of, 'Five-elevenish. Dark hair – well cut. Linen trousers – nice, subtle shade of khaki. Expensive polo shirt. Good body all over.'

'What was your name supposed to be again?' Denny whispered, quickening his pace.

'Miranda.' At least she'd been allowed to choose her own name. She'd plumped for one which sounded deliciously feminine but believable for a landlord's wife – at least in this part of the world.

'Mr Holme-Lacey?' Denny strode forward, holding out his free hand. 'Dennis Warner, remember? The Boatman's Rest.'

Holme-Lacey smiled. It was the sort of smile that said, Of course I remember. I remember everything. People who are in control usually do.

'It's Peter,' he said as he took Denny's hand. 'And I don't believe I've . . . ?'

'Oh sorry – this is my lovely wife, Miranda. You wouldn't have met her the other week.'

Holme-Lacey took Lia's hand. He had a strong handshake. He even hurt a little as he crushed the bones of her knuckles close together. She made an effort not to let him go too soon.

'I'm surprised a busy publican and his wife can

take a Saturday off at this time of year to visit a jazz festival.'

'I've got an excellent barman. He can hold the fort.'

'What's it worth not to tell Mike you said that?' Lia chipped in. 'He'll be asking for a rise.'

He laughed. Both men laughed. It was a good move. It said, We are in the same trade. We understand each other.

'No, seriously,' Denny went on – and she had to give him his due, he sounded very natural, 'I'm thinking of booking a few bands for the pub later in the summer. Just wanted to check out the talent. In fact, I've seen a manager just over there I need to touch base with. What about you, Peter? Business or pleasure?'

'Both. I'm still trying to catch the ladies I missed at your place.'

'Oh, are they here today?'

'They were supposed to be. We had an appointment – or I thought we did. Much more of this and I'll think they're trying to give me the slip.'

'I've just got to catch that band manager before he disappears again,' Denny said quickly. 'If you'll excuse me a moment . . .'

When he was gone, Peter turned to Lia and smiled. It was the sort of smile that was used to getting what it wanted.

'I'd like to buy you a drink while we're waiting for your husband – but would that sound gauche? Like a busman's holiday?'

She rolled the sound of his voice around in her head for a moment. It was an educated voice. Almost certainly public school educated. But not in the foppish, effete sort of way she usually associated with that type of man. It had a low, rich timbre. Talking with Peter – flirting with him – was hardly going to be a chore.

'I can always be talked into a very dry cider. Especially if it's chilled. Better make it a half at this time of day.'

He queued up at the beer tent. Lia watched him. He didn't have to stand and wait long, even though others had been there before him. He had the sort of presence that gets noticed. Who did he remind her of? The sort of mature actors she'd had mad crushes on when she was fourteen or so. That same air of authority.

While she was waiting, a table came free in the shade of a sycamore and she nabbed it. It was pleasantly cool with a breeze coming in off the river, but mainly she wanted the table to tuck her legs safely out of sight. Keeping her knees covered would be one less thing to remember.

'You're recently married,' Peter stated as he came up behind her, taking her by surprise as he set her drink down on the table.

'Why d'you say that?'

'One – I'd heard on the grapevine a couple of years back Dennis Warner was divorced. Two – the way he referred to you as 'my lovely wife'. I'm afraid we men don't stay that romantic for very long.'

'I've got my ways of keeping Denny on his toes.'

'I don't doubt it. Just make sure he doesn't work you too hard.' Peter reached across the table and stroked the curve of her right upper arm. 'You're developing barmaid's biceps already. Not that I think there's anything wrong with muscular women. On the contrary. Strong, well-toned women are very sexy.'

Her deception was that convincing? His comments took her off guard for a moment. And then she almost chuckled at the rightness of it. Of course, fifteen months of guiding the *Lady Jayne*'s tiller, winding up the lock mechanisms, pushing open the heavy lock gates and hauling on the barge's tow rope must have given her superbly toned arms – as well as the pecs and cleavage Denny had complimented her on.

He might have touched her arm but that wasn't where his gaze rested. Trudi had been right. The little art nouveau fairy fake tattoo nestling in her cleavage was an irresistible attention getter. Lia capitalised on the moment, leaned forward across the table and crossed her arms under her breasts before saying, 'Did I hear you say you were after those girls who run Straight and Narrow Catering?'

'Yes. Business. It's a bit complicated.'

Lia picked up her cold cider glass. In the heat, condensation had gathered on the outside. She ran the tip of her tongue carefully, slowly backwards and forwards across the rim a few times before she took a sip. There was a tiny drip of crisp, ever so slightly sparkling cider left when she'd finished. She flicked it up with her tongue very deliberately. The action managed to drag Holme-Lacey's attention away from her cleavage. And he shifted in his chair as if something was uncomfortable all of a sudden.

'They're nice kids,' she ventured. 'And very popular with the punters. Our trade doubles whenever they pull up. Of course, Denny and I do bar snacks all the time. Who doesn't, these days? But what those girls can rustle up in that little galley – that's something else. Did you want to book them for one of your functions?'

'It's more complicated than that. And I'm not sure if I should really ...'

'Come on. Don't be so secretive.' Lia slid a finger under the almost insignificant shoulder straps of her vest top and rubbed her fingertip up and down as if trying to scratch an itch. In doing so her neckline slipped a little further south, along with his gaze. 'It's not as if I don't know them, after all.'

'Well ... Don't tell anyone I told you. But I'm their landlord now. If a boat can have a landlord. I need to catch up with them to discuss terms.'

'I thought they were independent.'

'They certainly act that way. But no. The boat itself used to belong to some batty old aunt or great aunt or fairy godmother of one of them.' Here, Lia's jaw clenched. *She* might be allowed to take the mickey out of Auntie Faye but not anyone else. 'Anyway, she got into financial difficulties, as batty old ladies on their own tend to do. So she sold me the boat. Only, I'm not as inclined to treat the whole thing as a charity case.'

'Go easy on them. It is a new business.'

'Precisely. Which is why they need some guidance from an experienced older man.'

As he said this a shiver went through Lia's lower belly. There was an edge in the warm tone of his voice that made her wonder if he did just mean business plans and balance sheets.

'This flitting all around the country, for example,' he went on. 'It's so inefficient on fuel and so on. They need to focus their efforts.'

'I've always thought it must be one hell of a life. You know – nomadic. Never a chance to get bored. I envy them sometimes.'

'Hmm, and a husband in every port. Or whatever. Like the old sailor thing turned on its head. Don't look so shocked. I've heard rumours.'

He made eye contact for a change. She studied him closely. It wasn't just the air of confidence he had about him. His angular features were growing on her. The lean cut of his jawline. The thin line of his lips. Normally she preferred fuller, more sensual lips on a man. Peter's looked determined, but – just possibly – with the potential to be cruel.

'What will you do when you find them?' she asked. Her voice caught a little as she spoke. Not the confident, sexy role she'd cast for herself.

He smiled. 'You won't trip me up that easily. Let's just say I'm going to make them an offer they'd be very silly girls to refuse. If they're friends of yours, I don't mind you repeating that.'

He leaned back in his chair for a moment and twisted round to look at the riverside. 'That's where they said they'd be mooring up. And they should have been here by now. If they're giving me the run around they're making a very big mistake.'

His tone had hardly changed, he still sounded suave and charming. But there was ice beneath the surface.

'You'd better give me your number. In case I hear anything.'

'I gave your husband one of my business cards the other week.'

'Give me another. Just to be on the safe side.'

He reached into his trouser pocket for his wallet. Lia found it difficult not to stare, curiously, as he did so. He took out a top-quality printed business card and handed it to her across the table. Their hands met as she took it. Neither of them made an effort to draw away.

It was the slightest touch. Nothing more than polite social contact. But it made every cell in her tingle and sing out, drawn to his body as iron filings are drawn to an electromagnet when the current is turned on. It was a long time since she'd been this aroused by the merest brush of hands. But then, Peter was unknown territory. The thrill of the new possessed her. And he was her enemy. That gave it extra spice.

A crazy notion filled Lia's head. She wanted to keep hold of his hand, rise up and lead him along the riverside path. She knew, from having worked here the previous year, that after a few hundred yards the path entered a stretch of shadowy woodland. She wanted to take him there, press her body against his, against the thick, ridge-barked trunk of a fallen willow.

Right now she could feel his gaze as a warm, almost tactile thing, slipping down her cleavage. She wanted to feel his breath there too and then his lips. She wanted him to undress her, roughly and carelessly, against that tree with the deep-cracked bark biting into her bare skin. She wanted his dominant, bullish cock to enter her. And Peter's would be dominant – she was sure of that. But the need was insane. The auburn wig would slip, the patchwork of her untanned flesh would show and this whole thing was out of control. She tensed her stomach muscles tight against such savage feelings.

'It could be to your advantage,' Peter murmured, dragging her back to reality, 'if I persuaded those three to lead a more settled life instead of gypsying their way all over the Midlands. Put it this way: you imply they're your friends but I wouldn't turn your back on that new husband of yours while they're around.'

'Oh, I don't know.' She slipped her middle finger out of his grip and began teasing her fingertip in circles around his palm. 'If Denny plays away now and again it leaves me free to my own devices.'

'You're quite a woman, Miranda. If I was your husband I don't think I'd be leaving you to go off chasing band managers for quite so long.'

Lia shrugged and checked her watch. She was genuinely surprised to see how much time had passed.

'I didn't realise it was so late. Must be the company.'

'I'll take that as a compliment. But unfortunately it's late enough for me to assume I've been stood up.' Again, that cold undercurrent seeped into his voice. 'I hope I'll see you soon, though. And do call me. Whether you've heard any news or . . . whatever.'

He gave her hand a final squeeze and got up to leave. He didn't look back as he sauntered across the car park. Lia felt insulted. If she'd created an impression shouldn't he have glanced over his shoulder for a final sight of her? But men don't. Especially alpha-male types like Peter Holme-Lacey.

She watched him climb into a four-wheel drive. She didn't catch the make but she memorised its registration number and scribbled it down on the back of his business card. It might come in handy.

'Whew!' Denny bounded up and plonked himself down in the chair opposite her. 'Thought the coast was never going to be clear for me to come back. Well? Did you learn anything?'

And had she? Lia was forced to admit she didn't know any more about his plans. No more than she could have guessed. But he was no longer a shadowy figure. She'd met him, she'd got a handle on him, and all without giving herself away.

'I'm not sure,' she said at last. 'But I'm glad I let you talk me into it.'

'So I have my uses? And the other one is giving you a lift back to the boat. Ready?'

They got up and began side-stepping through the ever-swelling crowd. Denny took advantage of the crush and slipped his arm round her waist, pulling her close against him.

'I rather like the idea of you being my wife. Means I can tell you what to do.'

'And just what century are you living in?'

'Mind you, you're a naughty wife, flirting with another man in public like that. I should come down on you with a firm hand.'

He withdrew his hand from her waist and gave her a couple of experimental slaps on her buttocks. Denny had never done anything like that to her before. In the thin summer skirt she felt his smacks all too keenly. Coming hot on the heels of her sudden, frustrated arousal, courtesy of Peter Holme-Lacey, she felt acutely disappointed she wasn't going back to Denny's tonight.

'Hmm, hang on to that thought till the next time I'm in town.'

They were at Denny's car by now. His eyes met hers over the top as he unlocked it and he whispered, 'We could stop off somewhere along the way.'

It was so, so tempting. With the schedule they had lined up over the next few weeks it was going to be a long time before she saw either Denny or Jonathan again. And – despite whatever gossip Holme-Lacey might be having wet dreams over – she couldn't foresee getting laid for quite some time.

But his remarks about her being an inefficient business woman stung. She was damn well going to show him. And to do that she needed to get back to the boat.

'Keep it warm for me,' she said as she slipped into the car, leaned over to Denny in the driver's seat and gave his blue-jeaned thigh a squeeze. 'Right now I've got a business to run.'

About ten miles down-river, Trudi and Jules had – under Jules's direction – been spending the day serving up felafel in pitta bread and other vegetarian specialities outside a craft fair.

Denny pulled up in the car park near the *Lady Jayne*. But when Lia made to open the passenger door, he put a hand on her arm. 'Stay a moment. There's something I wanted to say.' He sighed and paused for a moment. Lia frowned. He was sounding serious – for Denny. 'That business about you pretending to be my wife brought it all back. You know she left me, don't you?'

Lia nodded. 'I was beginning to wonder if the plumber who put in all your wonderful bathroom fittings had anything to do with it.'

'Don't. That's not funny. There I was working my balls off downstairs to build up the business, and she was upstairs with that plumber working out the exact height the towel rail should go so she could hang on to it while he shagged her brains out. But no, it wasn't him she left me for. It was some nine to five computer programmer who used to drink in the pub. She got fed up with the long hours I was working. I expect she's got all the "quality time" she wants, now.'

Lia leaned over and nuzzled his neck. 'Maybe

she's got lots of quality time but I'll bet you anything she hasn't got such quality sex.'

He chuckled. 'You know how to cheer a man up. But seriously. It made me realise I probably don't have time for a full-time relationship. But what you and I have got – it's special, Lia. I want to know you're coming back.'

'What's brought this on? Just 'cause I was flirting with Peter Holme-Lacey? As if. Course I'll be back. You're my postman, remember?'

She kissed him. It was meant to be a quick kiss but it turned into something fiercer. Only a loud wolf whistle – it had to be Trudi's – from the nearby barge broke the mood.

'See you,' she whispered, swung out of the car and hurried towards the boat. And there was a particular swing in her step. Fond as she was of Denny, and deeply as she lusted after his masculine body, there was something exciting about being back with her mates and being on the move again.

'Well?' called Jules through the hatch. 'You're looking pleased with yourself. What happened?'

Lia paused a moment before she answered. In truth, she was feeling more pleased with herself than she had a right to be – especially as she hadn't found out any details about Holme-Lacey's plans. So where had this heady feeling of being on top of the situation come from? She had to be honest with Jules and Trudi. They'd agreed that. But it didn't mean she couldn't spin.

'He didn't rumble me,' she said, stepping down into the galley. 'I'm sure of that. And he still believes the itinerary that's up on the web site is the real one. So he's not hot on our trail. But he does want to meet with us. Badly. To "discuss terms" as he put it. He wouldn't give me any fine details but he'll want more of a slice of the action than Auntie Faye did. And to keep us in one place. I think he wants us where he can see us.'

'He can stuff that.'

'Precisely. Well, I know what he looks like now, how to handle him, and I've got his car registration and all his contact numbers. The more info we have, the more control we've got over the situation. At the moment I still think we're ahead.'

She paused and untangled herself from the long red wig. She was sure her own hair must look a sight – limp and sticking to her scalp with sweat. 'I won't be sorry to see the back of that, though!'

'Careful!' Trudi snatched it from her – over-protectively, Lia thought. 'It's got to go back in one piece.' Then she mellowed. 'But I'll tell you something. Jules is right. You do look . . . glowing.'

'It's the fake tan.'

'No. Seriously. You've got that sexy look of success about you. Or maybe it's the tattoo.' She placed a fingertip on the little fairy peeping out of Lia's cleavage. 'It does look sexy on you. Maybe you should get a real one done.'

'And maybe someone should give me a hand with this,' Jules interrupted, turning back to frying felafel on the gas griddle.

'Give me a moment,' Lia promised, 'then I'm all yours.'

She dumped her stuff in the cabin, then Trudi set her chopping fennel for the salad garnish.

'Yeuch,' Lia commented. 'Raw fennel. It's like celery. Too bloody worthy.'

'Don't knock it till you've given it a chance.' Trudi picked up a crescent of chopped fennel from the board and offered it to Lia's lips.

Lia hesitated for a moment. There was something unnerving about Trudi offering her food – which was crazy, considering they tasted each other's recipes all the time. But Trudi's fingertips were so very close to her lips. And Jules was close by, glancing over her shoulder as if expecting something to happen.

Lia parted her lips and accepted the slip of fennel. Trudi kept her fingers there for a moment, as if laying them over Lia's mouth to silence her. The sharp aniseed flavour prickled her taste buds. Then, as she began to chew, a warmth invaded her whole mouth. A surprising, sensual warmth. It wasn't worthy at all.

'I'll convert you yet,' Trudi murmured, reading the look on Lia's face.

And then the moment was broken as someone's mobile began to ring.

'Good,' Trudi commented, reaching for it. 'Should be that supplier getting back to me.'

'No – wait a moment.' Lia grabbed her arm. 'Check caller display before you answer.'

She scrabbled for Holme-Lacey's business card, which she'd left it on the side. Trudi held up the warbling phone. Sure enough, Holme-Lacey's land line number came up on the display.

'Leave it,' Lia hissed. 'Let the message minder cut in.'

The phone went silent after a couple more rings.

'We'll have to speak to him sometime,' Jules said.

'Yes, but I'd rather put a few more miles between us first. Soon as we've finished here I vote we head for Leamington.'

To her relief the others both nodded. Their next

booking was for another week at a country pub just outside Leamington Spa. The sort of venue that was popular with affluent weekenders from London at this time of year. They were always rushed off their feet when they cooked there. They were on strong territory. Maybe that was the place Holme-Lacey should be summoned to see them in action.

The evening light was mellowing when the last of the punters drifted away from the craft fair, and the girls decided it was time to cast off and make the most of the daylight left to them. Jules volunteered to steer. Lia headed for their cramped shower to try to scrub off the fake tan whose patchwork pattern was beginning to annoy her.

'It won't last long,' Jules called through the hatch after her. 'It was only cheap stuff.'

Trudi picked up a dishcloth to start on the clearing up but then seemed to think better of it. 'Bet you wish you were back in Denny's big bathtub. In more ways than one. If you want some help scrubbing your back you only have to ask.'

Lia turned at the shower cubicle door. Trudi was standing very close to her now. She was very aware of her height, her dominance, the way she was beginning to respond to Trudi as if a man were standing there.

'There isn't enough room for two. I'm sure you and Jules have found that out before now. You never give up, do you?'

Trudi winked and flashed her large, even, white teeth with the tiny gap between them that made her less than supermodel perfect but dazzling all the same. 'No. Because one of these days I'm going to catch you in the right mood. And you know it.'

CHAPTER

4

Lia woke early and took her coffee out on deck before anyone else was up. She loved this time of day. The air was cool, still a little dew-damp, and no one else had had a chance to use up its freshness. And there were muffled giggling noises coming from the bunks in the other cabin. She'd better leave them to it.

Trudi had seduced Jules before their first week at catering college was out. Lia remembered it well. Most people assumed that Jules, the bona fide lesbian, would have made the running, but no, Trudi was the predatory one. But remarkably untouched by jealousy. Sharing lovers with either Jules or Lia had never bothered her one bit.

What were they doing in that bunk right now? Lia felt more curious than ever before. The thought of two women together had never sparked more than a vague frisson but now it was beginning to turn her on. Not Jules, as such. She loved Jules in a friendly, sisterly way. She loved to hug her and feel that little head with its spiky, all-attitude hair against her cheek. She didn't feel desire, though: she never had.

But Trudi was something else. For a long time her physical closeness had made Lia feel on edge. She recognised that edginess for what it was now. And, with the prospect of not seeing either Denny or Jonathan for some weeks, the "right mood" was definitely stirring. But what to do about it? How to send out the right signals? How to flirt with another woman?

The anticipatory feeling stayed with her as the day wore on. They cast off again and Trudi stayed up on deck to help with the lock gates.

Jules went below to start on the VAT return – or perhaps she'd picked up on an atmosphere.

It felt good to be on the move. Exciting. Even if the *Lady Jayne* could only manage four knots, it still felt like a predator-and-prey game. Only Lia wasn't sure which was which. They were ducking and weaving from Peter Holme-Lacey. But at the same time she felt absurdly hunter-like. And the closeness of Trudi's body, just the other side of the tiller, sent a fizzy sensation through her blood.

'Watch your speed,' Trudi muttered. 'Those old blokes on the bank are glaring at us as if they're wondering where our water-skier has gone.'

'Let them.'

'What's got into you today? There are rules on the canal, Lia. Ease up.'

Reluctantly Lia pulled back on the throttle. She hadn't realised how fast she'd been going.

'I reckon that bit of play-acting yesterday went to your head,' Trudi continued. 'You've been in a funny mood ever since. Reckless.'

'And since when have you been Ms Sensible?'

'Hey!' Trudi grabbed the tiller from her and yanked it to one side. The lumbering barge responded only just in time. 'You nearly had us into the bank then. Concentrate, woman. You're dangerous today.'

'Good. I feel dangerous.'

Their eyes met. Both of them still had their hands on the tiller – close, but not quite touching. Lia flexed her fingers and stretched them out along the sun-warmed metal shaft. They were only millimetres away from Trudi's.

'You're still wearing my top from yesterday,' Trudi observed. 'It suits you.' She ran a finger along Lia's neckline. 'You should show a little cleavage more often.'

Lia's left hand tensed on the throttle. Their speed crept up again and she could hear the *Lady Jayne*'s bow wave wash against the canal bank. That was definitely against the rules.

'Show off,' Trudi said, reaching across, laying her hand over Lia's on the throttle and easing it back again. 'Don't forget, I've known you a long time. I've watched you playing up to men. I know when you're trying to impress one. Trouble is, I don't see any men standing close by.'

'Who do you see?'

Trudi didn't answer. But leaning over to take the throttle had brought her face right up to Lia's. Her lips were very close. They were plump and well rounded. Trudi licked them slowly. It was a calculated action, Lia thought. It made them glisten like an invitation. What would another woman's lips feel like on her own?

A klaxon sounded. She didn't get the chance to find out.

Trudi and Lia sprang apart. A large pleasure cruiser was heading straight for them. They'd drifted to the wrong side of the canal.

Lia heaved on the tiller. Too late. They were heading for the right-hand bank again, but a barge doesn't respond immediately like a car. And she'd been too heavy on the tiller in her haste to get them out of the way of the pleasure cruiser. She tried to get control back but they were caught in the larger boat's bow wave. They hit the concrete at the edge of the towpath with a sickening crunch and rebounded into the middle of the canal. Then they came to a stop with a sudden lurch and Lia and Trudi were thrown into each other's arms.

There was a strangled expletive from the galley and Jules emerged holding the side of her head. 'What the fuck's happening?'

'I think we hit a sandbank,' Trudi explained.

Lia realised Trudi was trying to cover for her. 'Maybe we did,' she admitted. 'But it was my fault. I wasn't . . . concentrating.'

They looked around and took stock. The *Lady Jayne* was listing in the water but she didn't seem to be holed. There was damage to the hull along the side but it seemed superficial and, at the angle they were leaning, above the waterline for the time being. But when they tried to start the engines again, to float her off, all they got was a metallic shrieking sound that set everybody's nerves on edge.

They were stuck fast in the middle of the canal. It was too far to jump. Trudi called to a couple of dog walkers on the towpath, threw them the ropes and they tried to pull the barge closer to the side. It was a futile exercise; the *Lady Jayne* was going nowhere.

'Better phone the fire brigade,' Jules muttered, picking up her mobile.

Trudi seemed to brighten. 'Mmm, hunky firemen. Best news I've had all day.'

Jules glared back at her. 'Grow up.'

There was a prickly silence as they waited for help to arrive. Lia and Trudi stuffed emergency clothes and overnight things into rucksacks and holdalls. Jules gathered the accounts she'd been working on.

When two fire engines drew up on the road beside the towpath, Trudi nudged Lia. 'What about the guy in front? Could quite fancy going down on a fireman's pole, myself.'

Lia turned to her in disbelief. 'You don't get it, do you? This is serious. About as serious as it could get in any circumstances, never mind the fact we're supposed to be outmanoeuvring Holme-Lacey. And all you can think of is . . . mind you, I can see your point.'

'See his, more like. Those safety harnesses are rather crotch-friendly.'

'Shut it, both of you,' Jules snapped without looking up from studying the map.

A cage on a crane lowered itself slowly over the towpath. One by one they clambered aboard and were lifted back to dry land. The young fireman Trudi had first spotted helped Lia over the rail and back on to solid tarmac. He did have a cheeky grin, she had to admit. And a certain air about him that only men who do something very physical and dangerous for a living possess.

Getting all three girls clear of the *Lady Jayne* took

the best part of an hour. Then the men turned their attention to the barge.

'It's a hazard where it is,' the commanding officer stated. 'You'll need specialist moving equipment to shift it.'

Jules produced Holme-Lacey's business card. Lia hadn't realised she'd rescued it from the boat. 'I'm going to phone the barge's owner. Tell him what's happened.' She turned and glared at Lia. 'Don't look at me like I'm a traitor or something. It's his property and he's got a right to know. Plus, he's probably the only one who can help us now.'

Lia didn't say anything. Because Jules was absolutely right. And the whole fiasco was her stupid fault.

Jules walked a little way down the towpath. After about ten minutes she came back and said, 'Lucky for us this guy seems to have contacts. A recovery barge will be here within the hour. I'll stay and wait for it. Time someone acted responsibly round here.'

Trudi reached over and touched her arm. 'But you hit your head when we crashed. You need to get it checked out.'

Jules shook off her hand. 'I'm fine. And if you had to crash the boat, Lia, I suppose we should be grateful you crashed it near a town with a mainline station.' She unfolded the map again. 'Don't know about you two but I'm getting the train to Jonathan's till this is sorted. At least I can use his PC to update the accounts and stuff while we're waiting.' She stomped off alone.

They were still glaring at each other in a kind of impasse when the young fireman walked up to them. As he spoke Lia realised he had a very slight

Welsh accent, which was far sexier than she would have expected.

'Sorry to interrupt, ladies, but I thought you should know. One engine's got to stay here until the recovery barge arrives but the rest of us have got to get back to the station. Strictly speaking we're not supposed to do this, but under the circumstances can we give you a lift anywhere on the way?'

Lia and Trudi turned and looked at the *Lady Jayne* again. Lia had been avoiding doing this. Their faithful, lovely barge was still listing at an undignified angle. 'The circumstances' hit Lia full on; the *Lady Jayne* wasn't just their transport, their place of work, but their home as well. She was homeless and jobless with just the contents of her rucksack to her name.

'We could all go to Jon—' she began but Trudi kicked her swiftly in the Achilles tendon.

'There's nowhere, really.' She did everything except flutter her eyelashes – which didn't go well with her five-nine height anyway – at the young fireman. 'At least nowhere we could reach tonight.' She glanced at her watch. It was nearly four o'clock.

The young man's grin widened. He had the most tantalising dimples when he did that, Lia realised.

'So you're looking for somewhere to crash tonight? Sorry – didn't mean to mention "crash". Hop in with us. We'll sort you something . . .'

His name was Jamie, they found out on the drive back to the station. Trudi was acting like a giggly child being allowed to ride in a fire engine. Lia had to admit her enthusiasm was becoming infectious. She might be making the best of a bad situation, but what the hell. They might have only a few hours before they had to face the music, big time. Tomorrow could look after itself.

The girls were dropped off at a house in the next street from the fire station.

'Make yourselves at home,' Jamie told them. 'Stick a pizza in the oven, if you like. My mates and I will be off shift in an hour or so.'

Trudi flung herself down on the sofa and laughed. 'Wonder if his mates are as good looking? And how many are there? "Mates", he said. Plural. So there's got to be at least three of them altogether. And only two of us. Could be interesting.'

'Trudi!'

'Lia, don't tell me you've never had a threesome.' She looked up and narrowed her eyes as if mentally flicking through all their college memories. 'No, I don't reckon you have. Well, well – nothing like a bit of spice to take your mind off things. Meanwhile let's get that pizza on. I'm starving.'

Trudi never seemed to need to watch the calories, Lia thought ruefully as her friend bit into the cheese-laden pizza with obvious delight. Her big frame could carry it off. And besides her enthusiastic sex life burning off the calories, she did her best to keep in shape; even aboard the barge she managed to do sit-ups and weights every morning.

'It's like that in South Africa,' she'd once explained to Lia. 'Because it's so hot and we wear such skimpy clothing everyone takes care of their bodies more.'

There was no getting away from Trudi's skimpy

clothing. Fed, relaxed and safe – for the moment – Lia felt a stirring. The mood she'd been in before the crash was rising again.

But Trudi leaped up from the sofa. 'I've often wondered about firemen's uniforms. Let's see if they've got any stashed away anywhere.'

'Trudi, we hardly know them! We can't go rooting . . .'

But Trudi had found a jacket and helmet in the cupboard under the stairs. She stripped off quickly, down to her glossy black matching bra and briefs. Lia had seen that set before – many times. They were used to washing their clothes together. It wasn't the most up-front sexy underwear Trudi had, but there was a sensual, silky feel to it. She'd felt it in the washing bowl, slippery with 'gentle care' liquid. What would it feel like with Trudi's warm body filling it out?

'I'd heard you were developing a uniform fetish,' she murmured as Trudi paraded before her in the thick jacket and helmet.

'I'm always open to new persuasions. What do you reckon? Sexy?'

Lia had to nod. The jacket came to the very tops of Trudi's long brown thighs and the dark colour next to her skin looked stunning. More than that, it lent her an aura of power. Of domination.

'We should have a camera,' Trudi said. 'You could take a picture of me doing a sly flash.'

She opened the jacket wide. She was still wearing the glossy, translucent bra and briefs set, but the sexual come-on of the pose was unmistakable. Trudi was prancing about like a glamour model and loving every minute of it.

Then the front door opened.

Jamie walked in followed by two other young men around the same age, one dark, one blond. Trudi didn't so much as blink.

'Oh,' she said, eyeing up their jeans and T-shirts. 'You've changed back into civvies. Spoilsports. I was looking forward to getting a better look at you in uniform.'

The firemen were caught on the back foot for a moment. Then the dark-haired one to Jamie's left said, 'If you're that interested in fire-fighter's equipment I've got some mountain rescue stuff I could show you in my room.'

Giggling and still wearing the borrowed jacket and helmet, Trudi ran before him up the stairs.

Lia shrugged and looked at the other two firemen. 'She's always been a bit mad, my friend,' she felt she had to explain. 'A good mate, though,' she added and it sounded a bit lame even as she said it.

And what about the way the two young men were looking at her? Did they think she was as easy? Was she?

Jamie broke the mood first and went to the kitchen. There was a sound of beer bottles clinking as he took them out of the fridge. The other young man – she thought she'd heard Jamie call him Ross – squatted by the stereo and put on a CD. It was instrumental. Some kind of Celtic–African rhythmic fusion. Lia sat stiffly on the sofa. The music was getting to her, though. The low, insistent beat wormed its way into her, kept time with her heart. Instinctively she began to move her shoulders in time.

Ross sat down beside her. Jamie came back with opened beer bottles for all three of them and sat on the other side. The sofa was small for three people and she could feel the warmth from their bodies seeping from their upper arms into hers. She was very aware of their proximity. And the beer had begun to relax her. That and the swirling, sensuous music.

Now and again the CD went quiet. Then the sounds from upstairs filtered through. Trudi wasn't giggling any more; she was moaning and squealing like a woman in the throes of sexual bliss. Even Lia hadn't heard her let rip like that before. On the barge, she and Jules normally kept a lid on things.

The sounds of someone else enjoying sex – and enjoying it so very enthusiastically – made Lia uneasy. She realised she was jealous. But jealous of the fact that Trudi was having sex, or jealous of the fact she was having it with someone else?

The musical emphasis shifted. The unremitting African drums were still pounding out their low rhythm, but a mischievous, playful flute was twirling high above them. It made her feel mischievous, too. And it made her feel like dancing.

Spontaneously Lia kicked off her sandals, got to her feet and began swaying and sashaying round the room. It was good to have this much space to move. This much space all to herself. In clubs she was hemmed in by the press of bodies. She never had the luxury of making up her own expansive, creative dance. She had the freedom now. And it didn't matter that Ross and Jamie were watching her and smiling – in amusement or approval, she didn't care which.

After the next track Ross got up to join her. She liked the way he moved, barely a foot away from her. He kept time to the drumbeat and his body was relaxed, going with the flow. She'd always firmly believed a man who was unselfconscious about his dancing was a man who was likely to be just as uninhibited in bed.

She studied Ross as they moved, mirroring each other's actions. He didn't have the same boyish charm as Jamie, true. But there was something so touchable about his blond, cropped hair. And his solid, very masculine body, beneath the tight, blue jeans and loose, black T-shirt, held promise. She could tell his shoulders were wide and muscular and his stomach toned and washboard flat. She'd never had a man who did anything quite so macho for a living. This could be interesting.

Trudi and her adventures upstairs were completely driven from Lia's mind. She moved a step closer to Ross, reached up and stroked his bleached crop. He put his hands on her hips and drew her closer still until their bodies were touching. At the same time Jamie got up from the sofa and moved behind her. He pressed against her from the rear.

For another slow-grinding track they continued to dance. All the time, Ross's big hands on her hips were pressing her closer to him. He was so much taller than her that they couldn't stand pelvis to pelvis. But she could feel the hard bar of his erection pressing into her stomach. And behind her, Jamie pressed closer too. He reached round, slipped his hands into the tight space between her and Ross, and cupped her breasts. In the skimpy little top she'd borrowed from Trudi there was no way she could have worn a bra. Her breasts were responsive in his hands. She moaned as he found her nipples through the thin material. The sounds of her pleasure seemed to turn him on. She could feel his growing swelling against her buttocks. Lia was surrounded by a tide of masculinity ready to be let off the leash.

Without speaking, they began to undress her. The music continued and their bodies, almost still, responded to it as Ross slipped Lia's scanty top up and over her head. As her breasts bobbed free he bent down and began to kiss them. Jamie's hands were still roving. Lia sighed in deep pleasure and leaned her weight back against Jamie's reassuring solidity as both men's fingers and lips moved over her breasts, vying to turn her on.

Where was this heading? She didn't care. It was growing dusky outside and the failing light wrapped them all up in a blanket. There was something intimate about the dimness; something liberating. Anything could happen.

Ross kissed his way down the front of her body, lingering at her belly button, which made her shiver with delight. He eased down her favourite purple skirt. For a moment she worried about whether the tanned and untanned bits still showed but what Ross did next drove everything except thoughts of pleasure from her head. He pressed his face against the thin, satiny triangle of her dark briefs and inhaled deeply. He was clearly turned on by a woman's scent. His arousal, his obvious appreciation, sent her own soaring. And not only that – his frantic breaths created delicious whirls and eddies of sensation all along the tender skin of her inner thighs.

Lia was becoming impatient; greedy for sexual release. Jamie was still behind her and his hands were rougher now on her bare breasts. The whole of her lower body was buzzing with tension.

Finally Ross peeled down her briefs. Lia gasped as she felt her swollen labia exposed to the air. This was what she wanted. Ross continued what he'd been doing through her panties, drinking in her warm, musky scent. The swirl of his breath through her pubic hair, hot one moment then cool as he breathed in, was incredible. But she wanted more. Her clitoris positively ached to be tongued. She opened her thighs a little and tilted her mons towards Ross, hoping he'd take the hint.

He did. His tongue slipped in between her juicy labia and flicked backwards and forwards in the warm, tender channel. At the end of each flick he circled her tense, pouting clit. He didn't keep it up long – just enough to keep her hanging there, slowly, slowly building towards orgasm. She was impatient but his tongue was controlling the pace. Lia's head reeled that such a man's man in a man's world should be so mind-blowingly good at oral sex.

She clenched her buttocks, thrusting her aching, horny quim into his face. Jamie pressed close behind her, reminding her his cock was horny too and wanting its release. Her thighs trembled. She wasn't used to coming standing up. The tensions in her body were unfamiliar and worked against each other. But that unfamiliarity added spice. For a time she wasn't sure how long she could keep this up but Jamie's hands grasped her breasts tighter and supported her.

Despite Ross's expert tonguing she wasn't as close to orgasm as she thought. Every time she wavered on the brink, the sensations seemed to ebb away again. The pent-up desire was driving her crazy. Lia strained her pubis towards his mouth, the muscles in her belly and her thighs locked tight. And then the longed-for orgasm ripped up through her – more intense, more deeply into her body than ever lying down. Her legs went weak and when the thumping in her sex had slowed to a delicious pulsing she sank to her knees on the floor.

Ross laid back on some scatter cushions before her. He unzipped his flies and took out his cock. There was no question about what she was going to do next. After he'd given her the most sublime cunnilingus, the only fair thing was to suck him off.

She eased down his flies still further and slid his tight, blue jeans out of the way so she could concentrate on his cock. It stood high in its coiled nest of reddish pubic hair. While not too long it was thick – stubby, in fact. Its meatiness had an eroticism all of its own. Lia covered its sensitive underside in kisses and mused that it would have been nice to feel this one inside her. Still, the night was young. She opened her mouth wide and took him in.

As she did so, she heard another pair of flies being unzipped. The very noise itself sent a shiver through her. Lia had always found the sound erotic and responded every time to the purring of a chunky brass zip and the promise that lay in wait behind it.

She was on her knees, virtually on all fours, to fellate Ross and her bare arse was poking high in the air. Jamie curled his body round hers. She felt his erection slip up and down between her buttocks. He was working himself in to a frenzy before he penetrated her.

He leaned forwards a little more, chuckled in her ear, and she could just imagine the dimples boyishly deepening in his cheeks as he began to talk dirty to her.

'We should tell all the lads down the station about you. About how you like it with more than one bloke at a time. What d'you reckon? Should we invite them all round?'

Lia couldn't answer. Her mouth was full of Ross's plump cock. He was thrusting it up towards her so forcefully she was glad he wasn't longer or she wouldn't have been able to take him all in. She moaned, low and enthusiastic, though, to let Jamie know she was enjoying the thought.

'I reckon we should,' Jamie continued. 'How many of them could you take? Would you bend over like you're doing now and let a whole shift of them give it to you from behind?'

The ambiguity of the phrase sent shivers all over Lia's body. In her mind, that most erogenous zone of all, the thoughts went wild. 'Give it to you from behind' – what did he mean? He probably meant no more than the sort of sex she and Denny had had in the bath that time. But it carried forbidden, wicked undertones of anal penetration. She'd never dared do that. She could fantasise, though.

'Or would you like to suck them all off? Something tells me you can't get enough cock. In your pussy, in your mouth . . . or wherever. And the look on Ross's face tells me you've got cock-sucking down to a fine art. Right, mate?'

She felt Ross's body shake as if he was nodding vigorously. She couldn't look up to see from where her face was buried in his lap. His prick felt full and meaty and very close to coming now. It was delectable between her lips; a delicious piece of flesh to pleasure.

And just at that moment, when her head was literally and figuratively full of cock, Jamie plunged his into her sex from behind. Lia drew in a sharp breath and her mouth tightened on Ross's swollen shaft. Jamie had entered her more decisively than she was used to – even with Denny. Her sex was juiced up after its divine tonguing and offered no resistance whatsoever. Still, the speed of his entry had taken her by surprise.

She turned her attention back to Ross's cock. She lolled her tongue up and down its most sensitive underside. She wanted him to come. She needed him to come and then she could concentrate on what Jamie's thrusts were doing to her. He felt big. He filled and stretched her and she wanted to focus her whole awareness where it deserved to be.

The blood was surging into Ross's erection now; she felt it pulse against her lips in readiness. And then he was coming in violent jets, filling her mouth with saltiness for a second before she swallowed it down.

Lia raised her head from Ross's lap. She was quite breathless now. She kissed his prick tenderly because she really loved the look, the taste, the texture of it under her lips. He took a long time to subside. Or perhaps he was showing the glimmerings of interest again.

Meanwhile Jamie's cock was pounding her sex. She loved the feel of its smooth, confident piston-action boring its way deep into the centre of her body. Every nerve ending in her vagina was dancing with pleasure. But it wasn't enough. Her clit was unrubbed at that angle and she wasn't close enough to coming. But Jamie was. She could hear it in the wildness of his breathing and feel it in the tension in his prick. Lia screwed her eyes tight shut and tried to fill her head with the dirtiest thoughts she could, but it was too late. Jamie bucked and spasmed inside her and roared in her ear as he came.

Her quim was still buzzing with the need for sexual release. But the men didn't seem to have forgotten that. They turned her over and lay her down on the floor. At any other time she might have balked at the thinness of the threadbare carpet but she was too excited by their threesome to care. She propped herself up on her elbows as the men began to feel her breasts again.

It was such a novelty having two pairs of hands roving over them at once. And such big, work-roughened hands. They seemed to overwhelm her. There was something verging on scary about being at their mercy. Because she was at their mercy; these two strong, well-built firemen could have done anything to her.

Jamie paused and sat up straight a moment to pull off his T-shirt. Beneath it his chest and shoulder muscles were thick and well formed. Lia had never gone in for body-building types before, but just being in a totally new sexual situation made her appreciate the warm curves of his deltoids and pecs. She reached up to run her hands over his chest and upper arms, and then Ross sat back and began to strip off too.

They had heavy thighs, both of them. And

sturdy hips – not the narrow, palm-filling buttocks she normally went for. Fleetingly she thought of Jonathan and a stab of tenderness went through her. Then she forgot him again in her excitement. Jamie and Ross were built for a different kind of action. She imagined those strong hips thrusting and those buttock muscles flexing as they drove relentlessly into her.

Ross reached forwards and began fondling her breasts again. The little fairy tattoo was still peeping at the top of her cleavage. Glancing down and seeing it there took Lia by surprise: yesterday's cloak-and-dagger games seemed a lifetime away. The men seemed fascinated by it, though, and with such a reaction, she began to wish it was real.

This breast adoration was bringing the rising hunger in her sex to overload. She writhed under Ross's dominant hands, and the little involuntary mewing noises she was making were begging him to take pity on her. And it was turning him on too; she could see his thick cock swelling again.

Lia parted her thighs. She was aroused already and eager to be taken. Without a word, Ross dipped his hips and entered her.

A warm wave of pleasure swept up her quim as he did so. She was close now, very close. With Ross on top of her, his big paws still planted on her breasts, she was getting stimulation in all the right places. His thick cock thrusting inside soon built her up to a deep, clasping orgasm.

He didn't break his rhythm for a moment, even as she screamed out in her pleasure. He kept on thrusting and it seemed to prolong those little pulsing sensations as the vehemence of her climax ebbed away. Her quim was tingling with post-orgasmic sensitivity, and as he carried on rough-riding her, she wondered if she was going to come again.

What of Jamie? Lia opened one eye just for a moment and, in the dimness, caught sight of him rubbing his cock lovingly. He'd had no trouble, it seemed, coaxing a second erection. The sight of another couple making it clearly turned him on.

Ross groaned loudly and she felt his warm, liquid explosion bursting her, filling her. Her own desire was rising again. She was greedy for another orgasm. But no sooner had Ross withdrawn than Jamie moved to take his place between Lia's thighs.

Much as she'd enjoyed being dominated, something clicked inside her head.

'Variety, guys,' she whispered, and twisted out of the way before Jamie could get his cock inside her. 'I don't like doing it the same way twice in succession. Lie down, big fella.'

That dimpled grin came back again as Jamie lay down among the big scatter cushions. A grin like that could melt many places inside her. She didn't doubt that it had got a few girls' juices going before now.

She gazed down on him for a few moments before she mounted him. Jamie had a superb body by anyone's standards. Not a spare scrap of flesh on him. Everything was hard and ready for action. And she meant everything. His prick was thick and longer than his colleague's. No wonder he'd felt so amazing inside her from the rear.

She lowered herself down and impaled her tender quim on a cock so firm it felt as if an iron bar were filling her. Lia was almost raw inside now from so much over-enthusiastic sex, but she couldn't stop. She was feeling so greedy. She made little rocking motions on top of Jamie. She knew they must be infuriating for him, but the root of his thick cock was nudging just the right spot: her hot clitoris.

Ross reached round from behind, cupped her breasts and began rolling her nipples. They, too, were raw and over-used. But Lia wanted everything. She didn't care what she might feel like tomorrow; tonight was a night for excess.

She had almost come to a standstill on top of Jamie. She had just the perfect action and perfect angle to spin her pleasure out for as long as she could bear. Maybe this was what they meant by mystical, tantric sex? But Jamie was writhing and bucking his hips in protest beneath her.

Lia eased the angle of her body forward a fraction, touched the trigger spot and another orgasm rippled up into her body. Three orgasms. She grinned. And all so different. Then she rode Jamie faster and faster, her sex burning with the furious friction until he thrashed beneath her and she felt him come.

When she rolled off, they all sank down together on the carpet. It was a sultry night and even with the sweat drying on her naked body she still felt warm. And the sheer poundage of masculinity on either side of her was enough to keep her warm on its own.

As drowsiness came and swallowed Lia up she vaguely noted the music was still going in the background. It must have been set on continuous play. Had that been a forethought?

CHAPTER

5

L ia awoke to the smell of coffee and someone saying, 'C'mon sleepyhead,' in her ear. It was a moment before she realised the voice was female and had the nasal trace of a South African accent.

She sat up and rubbed her eyes. She was lying naked on the sofa. Someone must have lifted her on to it and covered her with a duvet. She didn't remember that.

Trudi waved the mug under her nose. 'It's cheap and it's instant, but it's as good as you're going to get this morning. The boys have already left for work, by the way. So, give us the goss. You have both of them?'

Lia moaned as she stretched and took her coffee. 'Twice each. Ow. I feel like I did the morning after I lost my virginity.'

'In a way you have. But I'll tell you something, you haven't done threesomes properly till you've done them both ways – if you get my drift.'

Their eyes met. Lia felt a curious, fluttery feeling in her stomach. 'I'll bear that in mind.'

'Funny thing about threesomes,' Trudi continued, unperturbed, sipping her coffee. She was wearing a man's loose, white shirt, a little pair of black pants underneath and, very obviously, no bra. 'The dynamics are totally different when you've got two women as opposed to two blokes. I mean, when you had the two guys last night, I take it they kept their hands well away from each other? They didn't feel each other up or pleasure each other or anything?'

Lia thought back on it and laughed. The very idea of it. No, it hadn't occurred to her at the time but the thought of two such masculine males having anything sexual between them just didn't compute.

'Thought so,' Trudi continued. 'Now with girls it's anything but. Sometimes the guy hardly does anything at all, just lies back and gets off on watching the two of you loving each other up. But you don't have to take my word for it.'

No, she didn't. Lia was very aware that under the borrowed duvet she was still naked. There was a tightening in her groin. Trudi was so close now. The tension between them that had wrecked the boat yesterday was rising again. Only this time there was nothing to wreck.

They both put down their coffee cups at the same moment. Trudi slid her hands across the sofa and covered Lia's fingers with her own. When Lia didn't flinch away it was a turning point. A moment of surrender. Trudi leaned across and kissed her fully on the lips.

To Lia's surprise she made the next move herself, parting her own lips and snaking her tongue into Trudi's mouth. It just felt right. Softer, more sensual than a man's kiss. For a while they did nothing but explore each other's tongues. Trudi could stretch deep inside Lia – everything about her seemed larger than life – running her tongue-tip up and down the roof of Lia's mouth, exploring the inner edges of her teeth, filling her with a moist, warm, writhing sensation. There was no hurry.

Eventually it was Trudi who pulled back and began nibbling her way down Lia's neck. The duvet fell away. Lia's breasts were bare for the kissing.

'Tell me what happened,' Lia whispered between moans of pleasure, 'with you and that other fireman – whatever his name was – last night. No, don't stop that, though.'

Trudi chuckled. 'You want me to talk dirty to you? Hmm. Don't know what his name was. Never asked. But the stuff he had in his bedroom. Oh, you should have seen it, Li. All the harnesses and straps and stuff. Great for bondage. I made him strip off and just wear this abseiling harness. It cupped his dick and his balls and just made them, you know, stand out so obviously. A real feast for the eyes. Don't care what some women say, I like looking at a man's tackle. And the rope he had. Tons of the stuff. He tied me to the bed with it and came just about everywhere he could think of. And I do mean *everywhere*, Li. Just as well he had plenty of baby oil to hand but even so I'm sore this morning as well. Just in the right mood for a little softer loving . . .'

Lia reached for Trudi and cupped her breast through the soft, overwashed cotton shirt. Feeling another woman's big, firm but yielding breasts sent an illicit thrill through her.

'It must have been a hell of a night,' she whispered. 'Your nipples are going hard again just thinking about it.'

'I don't think that's anything to do with last night. That's you turning me on.'

Trudi had reached Lia's nipples by now. She kissed and flicked them with her tongue, making slow circling motions with the very tip. She was more controlled, more precise than a man could be. And she was in no hurry. She was infuriatingly in no hurry. Lia's desire was a rising, strangling feeling in her lower belly and she was impatient for Trudi to move on and satisfy her. She kicked the duvet right away and sank back on the sofa ready for a little further action.

But Trudi just chuckled again and murmured, 'You really have been doing it with men for far too long. What's the hurry? Sex isn't a race. What else do we have planned today?'

She leaned forwards over Lia's tummy and kissed a wide circle round her deep belly button. Round and round she kissed, setting Lia's nerve endings tingling. For several minutes she did nothing more than this.

'Beautiful,' Trudi murmured between licks and kisses. 'But you should think about getting yours done, too. Having a body bar in there is unbelievably sensual. Like right now, my tongue could be fiddling with it. That would blow your mind, Li. Piercing makes your flesh that much more sensitive to the touch. Take my word for it – it's awesome.'

Lia didn't answer. Trudi's tongue had snuggled itself right into her navel at long last. The swirl of sensations that warm, moist flesh provoked made her feel her belly button was almost another clitoris. Both knots of nerve endings were buzzing with diffuse sexual arousal. Not even Jonathan was this thorough with his oral attention.

Then Trudi began to kiss her way down over the very slight swell of Lia's lower belly and brushed her cheeks against Lia's tangled pubic hair. She didn't seem remotely bothered that only a few hours previously two men had come and come and come again in there. She eased her tongue between those warm sex lips and began to glide it up and down.

Lia gasped. There was a little tenderness still there but Trudi's ministrations were kissing it all better. Her labia felt like two delicious slips of steak she'd pummelled and tenderised ready to serve up to a special client. The rough riding they'd had the night before made them all the more responsive to Trudi's gentle kiss. Maybe there was something to this pleasure–pain thing. Maybe Trudi had a point about body piercing.

Relaxing back on the sofa and spreading her welcoming thighs as wide as they would go, Lia began to fondle her own breasts. She wouldn't have done this with a male lover. She would have felt too self-conscious. Sex with Trudi felt more sharing than she had ever imagined.

Warm snakes of pleasure tunnelled all through her lower body in time to Trudi's playful tongue. Another woman knew just what she should do – just the right pressure, just the right spot. Trudi must have done this so very many times. Lia smiled. And now she was reaping the benefits.

The tingles, stabs and wriggles of pleasure grew stronger the nearer to climax she came. Those particular waves of desire that only oral sex can prompt shivered up her vagina, closer and closer together now. They rolled into one long wave and the orgasm that welled up in her felt almost like a little animal burrowing its way deep into the very centre of her body. Lia convulsed in pleasure and almost lifted clear of the sofa. Trudi kept tonguing her gently until the last aftershock ripples of pleasure had dissolved away.

Lia sat up. It was her turn now. She wasn't wholly sure what to do. She leaned forwards and kissed Trudi again; her lips were more swollen, pillowy and sensuous than ever after their efforts down below. And she tasted strangely of the mixed sexual flavours: Lia's, the men's and her own very individual taste. All the while she was kissing her deeply, Lia reached out and began undoing the buttons all the way down Trudi's borrowed shirt. The blue crystal in her belly button seemed to wink suggestively. Those big, warm breasts slipped into Lia's hands. Lia took her time fondling them, marvelling at their texture, their combination of softness and strength, their kissable café au lait colour and outrageously dark nipples.

Just as she was about to take one in her mouth a mobile phone trilled down on the floor.

'Ignore it,' Lia hissed; Trudi had laid a hand on her hair as it to say, Stop.

They froze for a moment. The lazy, sensual mood was perilously close to being broken. When, after so many rings, the trilling cut off because the message minder had taken over, they both began to breathe again. Lia closed her lips round Trudi's prominent, hard nipple.

The phone began to ring again. Lia rested her head against Trudi's breast with a sigh.

'Someone wants to get hold of us badly, Li.'

'Yeah. I can take a guess at who.'

The phone went silent. But almost straightaway it began ringing again.

'I can't stand this,' Trudi snapped. 'I've got to answer it.'

The sexy mood was absolutely shattered. She'd pulled her shirt back round her and was scrabbling on the floor.

'Yeah? Jules? Oh, thank God, we thought it was ... Ah. I see. We're in Leamington itself.' She tucked the phone into her neck for a second and said to Lia, 'Look out the door, will you? See if you can read what street we're on and check what number while you're at it.'

'Oh sure, stark naked ...' Lia found something to wrap round herself and risked a quick peek outside. She came back and told Trudi what she wanted to know.

'Right,' Trudi relayed the information into the phone. 'Thirty minutes? Where the hell are you? Okay ... Okay. Looks like we don't have much choice.'

She broke the connection and sighed at Lia. 'Jules was phoning from some posh car Holme-Lacey had sent for her. They're on their way to pick us up. Time to face the music, kiddo.'

'Oh my God! He mustn't know it was me. I mean, he mustn't recognise me from the jazz festival the other day.' Lia slapped her forehead in a panic. 'Clothes! He's seen the ones I was wearing. No, it's okay, I should have some spare I rescued from the boat – where the hell did my rucksack go?

And this bloody tan. It's no good, I've got to grab a shower to scrub the last of it off. And this tattoo, it's a dead giveaway.'

She was attacking it with her fingernails when Trudi put a hand over hers to stop her. 'Those things come off a treat with baby oil. Upstairs. Just as well I had cause to discover some last night. Oh, and I'll leave a note for the guys while you're at it,' she called after Lia with a wink. 'After all, they were good to us!'

The car that drew up outside was an ice-white Mercedes. Several neighbours found cause to put their milk bottles out – one by one and thoughtfully – during the few minutes after it had purred to a halt. Still damp from her hasty shower, Lia rushed after Trudi and dived into the back seat while trying not to feel too self conscious.

Jules was already there. Being the smallest she moved into the middle to make room for them; Lia and Trudi were physically kept apart. Lia wondered if that had been calculated.

The tall, blonde chauffeur looked over her shoulder to make sure they were belted up but she said nothing. Her attractiveness was as glacial as the whiteness of the car, and in her uniform she seemed androgynous. There was an atmosphere in the back seat. No one said anything for the half hour it took to drive to Holme-Lacey's residence.

At that point Lia gasped. She couldn't help it. And it did seem to crack the frostiness in the car. Holme-Lacey's pad was a Georgian mansion in beautiful condition. They approached it slowly down a long, curving driveway which gave them every chance to admire the landscaped grounds that swept down to the river. As they drew up in front of the house itself Lia also spotted a massive conservatory – recently built, she assumed, but in perfect keeping with the rest of the architecture – that housed an indoor swimming pool. In the rear-view mirror she caught a glimpse of the chauffeur grinning smugly on her employer's behalf – or maybe he wasn't just her employer?

They were shown to a sun-filled morning room. There was a steaming pot of coffee on the table and several plates piled high with Danish pastries. Remembering they'd had no time for breakfast, Lia and Trudi pounced on them until their mouths and fingers were sticky with sweet fondant icing.

'How's Jonathan?' Lia asked Jules.

'Fine.'

And that's all they could think of to say to each other for the next twenty minutes. Eventually Trudi glanced at her watch and muttered, 'He's doing this deliberately. Power-waiting or whatever it's called.'

'If that's the case you'd better consider who I learned it from.'

Something prickled all over Lia's skin. That voice again. Rich and warm as the sun streaming through the south-facing windows, but with a hint of menace, dark as bitter chocolate. They turned and looked as Peter Holme-Lacey entered the room. The door had been ajar and there was no telling how long he'd been standing outside it.

'But we won't dwell on silly bygones,' he continued, moving further into the room and helping himself to the last Danish pastry the girls had all been too polite to claim. 'I asked you here to talk about the future.'

He looked coolly at each of them in turn. There wasn't a flicker of recognition as Lia felt his eyes lock on to hers. At least she'd got away with that. She licked jam and sugar frantically from the corners of her lips. Because there was something about him that made her feel like a nervous schoolgirl called to the headmaster's office, and right now she needed every psychological advantage she could get. Including trying to look like a grown up.

'The *Lady Jayne* is a bit of a mess,' he stated. 'I've just been to see her this morning. Finally.'

'It was an accident,' Trudi snapped. If her chair had been closer, Lia would have reached over and squeezed her hand in gratitude for her loyalty.

'Let's hope my insurers see it that way. You do realise I had the boat insured, don't you? She was my property, after all.'

Lia felt a stab. She hadn't thought about insurance and stuff like that. The *Lady Jayne* was their home. But it wasn't theirs.

'And as my property,' Holme-Lacey went on, 'if my insurers believe she was being piloted recklessly, they may want me to bring charges. But I'm sure it won't come to that.'

It was a warm morning and warmer still in that suntrap room. But Lia could feel her cheeks prickling with cold as the blood drained away from her face. She was glad Trudi was there to do the talking.

'What is it you want from us, mister?' Lia had often noticed how Trudi's accent became harder when she had to stand up to someone. Right now she was grateful for it.

'I want us both to have a successful business

84

relationship. One of those win-win situations. But I've made an investment. I expect a return on it. We'll draw up a proper leasing contract for the boat once these repairs are sorted out. That should take a few weeks. Once you're up and running again I should be in a position to put a lot of corporate entertaining your way. That's where the money's to be made. Not faffing around in pub beer gardens.'

He reached into an inner pocket of his pale, linen suit and drew out some papers. They looked, Lia thought, suspiciously like contracts.

'In the meantime,' he continued, 'we could do each other a favour. You all know who I am and I'm sure you know I host a lot of one-day conferences here. I still haven't found a firm of catering subcontractors in this area that I'm totally happy with, though. You could run that side of things until your boat's ready to go again. I asked my PA to draw up some contracts for that this morning.' He placed them carefully on the table in front of them. 'Don't look so appalled at the rates I'm offering, Ms Van der Plaas. I'm prepared to offer you board and lodging here for the duration, so I believe it all evens out.

'Oh – and you'll notice there are only two copies.' He looked at Jules. 'I believe I'll only need two of you and your predilections do rather argue against you being one of them.'

He paused, just long enough for Jules's face to turn dark with blood and her small, strong hands to crush the bamboo arms of her chair, before continuing, 'I understand from your web site that your particular speciality is ethnic vegetarian cuisine. There's not much call for that sort of thing among my business contacts. Of course, much misinformation has found its way on to your web site recently so correct me if I'm wrong . . .'

'It's not bloody fair!' Jules was on her feet in front of Holme-Lacey. Not that drawing herself up to her full five-foot-one height and planting her hands on her hips gave her that much of an advantage when facing him. 'I was the one who co-operated. I was the one who rang you when the boat got damaged. Is this how you treat people who try and play fair by you?'

Lia bunched her fists against her chest. Deep inside, she was cheering Jules on. Peter Holme-Lacey was a manipulative bastard. They should just tell him to shove his offer. But . . . he'd given them a way out. Face-saving. Somewhere safe to stay while this whole mess was being sorted. And it was only temporary.

'I know you rang me – probably against the wishes of your colleagues – and I'm truly grateful for that. But you can't afford to be sentimental in business. I hope you don't feel you've had a wasted journey this morning as I was concerned all three of your should hear what I had to say. Naturally my chauffeur will take you back to wherever you wish to go.'

He turned to Trudi and Lia. He smiled that smile again. The one Lia recognised from the jazz festival. The thin-lipped smile that brought the words 'constructively cruel' to mind.

'Forgive my manners,' he said, reaching into his jacket pocket again and taking out a black, lacquered fountain pen with gold trim. 'I didn't offer you anything to sign the contracts with.'

'Suppose we don't want to play ball?' Trudi demanded.

'That's your prerogative. But I could stick with my existing catering arrangements more easily than you can find a new boat in a hurry.'

Trudi's hand twitched on the paper for a moment. Lia didn't know which way she was going to jump. After one of those thirty second pauses that seem to last all day she muttered, 'Sorry, Jules,' and took the pen.

'When you two finally remember you have spines,' Jules hissed, 'you'll find me at Jonathan's. Goodbye!'

She slammed the door so hard, Lia was disappointed nothing expensive went tumbling to the floor.

CHAPTER

6

Lia wandered, barefoot, down the long, dark lawns that sloped towards the River Avon. Even after dark, summer was advanced enough now for warmth to linger thickly in the air, and the slight breeze coming off the river promised freshness. She hadn't been able to sleep.

After their rather one-sided meeting, Peter had disappeared for the rest of the day. She found herself thinking of him as 'Peter' and it pulled her up sharp. Labelling him 'Holme-Lacey' in her mind made him seem more at arm's length.

Trudi had taken herself off to her room to 'unpack'. Yeah, like it took all afternoon to unpack one holdall full of hastily grabbed clothes. Truth was, they were avoiding each other. Neither was proud of what they'd done.

She stopped and rubbed her bare sole against the grass. It was such a sensual feeling – the very fine, tickly blades just beginning to moisten with dew. Lia almost laughed. The whole thing was surreal. Her – barefoot on a croquet lawn under the stars. She'd be drinking Pimms and wearing ball gowns next.

There was a gazebo near the river. It had some lights strung up around it but no one was there. She made for it and enjoyed the coolness of running water for a moment. The river made a low, melodic, rippling song. But she knew it could be dangerous, too. Just like Peter. She meant Holme-Lacey.

In the darkness behind her, she heard a clink.

'Trudi? That you?'

It wasn't. The man who approached out of the shadows was carrying a wine bottle and two glasses.

'A chilled oaked Chardonnay,' he said, setting everything down on the gazebo bench between them. 'I understand that's what you trendy young things like. I hope it hasn't warmed up too much while I was looking for you.'

She wished they could turn back the clock. To the last time he'd offered her a chilled alcoholic drink beside a river and she'd licked the tiny drops of condensation off the rim and fantasised the hard glass was his yielding body.

But you knew he was a bastard then, she told herself. Every instinct warned you. Now he's just proved it by stitching you up and cutting out one of your best friends. But still . . . But still . . . she took the glass he offered her.

'Why us?' she said after a while. 'Why did you want us when you've got all this and probably a hell of a lot more I don't know about?'

'You can count on that. Want? I like to think I was doing your godmother a favour when I bought the *Lady Jayne*.'

'You don't do favours.'

He shrugged and smiled. 'Maybe I just liked the outrageousness of it: three kids barely out of college, thinking they can make a go of a catering business on a barge. In a funny kind of way I admire you. I think a lot of people do. I met a rather lovely lady the other day who told me she envied you.' He broke off for a moment and sipped his wine as if reliving a pleasant memory.

Lia allowed herself a little smirk. He wouldn't see it in this dim light. She'd got away with the deception. Small triumph now, of course, but it was still a heady feeling.

'Your turn,' he continued. 'Why a narrow boat?'

'It was cheaper than setting up our own restaurant. Have you any idea of the costs?'

'Of course. I'd bought and sold about half a dozen at the last count.'

'And I've always had this thing about canals ever since I was a kid. They're romantic. If you're brought up in a city they can be the only quiet, restful place. And do you know their history? They were so radical when they were built. Changed everything. And the people who worked on them were seen as dangerous. Unconventional. Outside the rules.'

Why am I doing this? she thought. I'm rambling. And on only half a glass of Chardonnay. He doesn't need to know any of this. My childhood dreams, my crazy romantic notions. It'll only let him get a handle on me and then where will we be?

'Things haven't changed so very much,' he said, and reached for her free hand. 'About the people who work on canals, I mean. They're still a little outside conventional society. Am I right?'

There it was again. Just the touch of his hand on hers sent a ripple of wanting up her forearm and shivering through the rest of her body. She still might think of Peter Holme-Lacey as 'the enemy'. Her hormones didn't.

'You're different,' he said as he raised her hand to his lips. 'From the other two, I mean. They're so prickly. But you and I can work together.'

She was being spun a line and she knew it. But it was nice to hear, all the same. And it didn't matter what he was saying. That smooth voice alone could seduce her. A voice with that much confidence in itself would convince anyone. She had no defence against it.

He pressed his lips against the inside of her wrist. It was such a sensitive place. The warmth of his breath met the warmth of her blood teeming just beneath the skin. Lia trembled. If touching her in such an innocent place could make her feel like this, she could barely trust herself. But did she want to?

'I'm not your enemy,' he whispered into her palm as though he'd read her previous thoughts, 'and I think you know that. This could be good.'

This? What did 'this' mean? Lia's head reeled between what he meant and what she wanted him to mean. He couldn't only be talking about business, not when he held her hand so ardently and his breath coiled around her skin. Whether she'd misjudged him or not became irrelevant. She wanted him. Working out the implications of that could wait till morning.

With a swift movement Lia knocked back the rest of her glass of Chardonnay. It was so crisp on the tongue, so fresh and subtly perfumed it was a shame not to savour it. But she had to say this now or she'd lose her nerve. And she wasn't going to finish the rest of the bottle and get herself into a state where she was easy prey. Peter mustn't think of her like that. She was a twenty-first-century independent woman with a business of her own, and he'd better remember it.

'Let's go inside,' she said. 'This close to the river the mossies are going to start biting soon.'

'Inside it is then,' he replied, stroking the outer curve of her bare arm. 'I'd hate to see this skin get bitten . . . by anything it shouldn't.'

She stood up to walk towards the house. But her ankle must have turned on an uneven patch in the dark grass and he caught her arm to save her from falling. And kept a firm hold of it.

'You've got beautiful arms,' he murmured, running the back of his fingers up and down the warm curve of her deltoid again. 'Reminds me of . . . someone. I like strong women. They're sexy.'

'Anyone would think you enjoyed being dominated.' That had slipped out. On only one glass of Chardonnay?

'Not in the least. But I don't like to win too easily. It spoils the fun. I know I said I wasn't going to rake up bygones but the way you and your friends led me a merry dance was quite exciting really.' He stopped in the middle of the dark, damp lawns and turned her forcefully towards him. 'It made meeting you all the sweeter in the end. And I knew I was going to. Sooner or later.'

She knew he was going to kiss her. But he took his time bending his head and pressing his lips to hers. All the while he was gripping the tops of her arms in a way that didn't exactly hurt, but she knew there was no escaping his hold.

His breath played over her upturned cheeks. The tiny, subtle caress prickled her nerve endings and sent eddies of sensation across her face, down her neck and into her dark cleavage buried in its summer top. Her insides seemed to melt, and she would have let him take her there and then on the lawns, never mind the dewy dampness, the grass stains or the mosquitoes ready to pounce on moist, bare flesh. He'd barely touched her. But she was ready to surrender.

All he did for a long moment, though, was to force his lips down on hers. They were hard and muscular – like the rest of him, she wondered? She'd never thought of lips as muscular before, but why not? They were the most mobile, expressive part of the human body. Right now, Peter's were moulding hers to their own shape as if he owned her. She wasn't used to being owned. Neither Denny nor Jonathan tried that. Peter's mature, overwhelming masculinity scared her a little. But the scariness was exciting.

He broke off. Her own lips felt bereft as he withdrew.

'Let's go inside,' he murmured in that rich, timbred accent of his, and there was absolutely no mistaking his intent.

Anticipation tightened her lower belly as they raced upstairs, down the long landing and into his room. Lia wasn't quite sure what she'd been expecting to find there. A dungeon of sexual domination games, perhaps? But it was quite an ordinary, if expensive and exquisitely furnished, bedroom. It figured. Peter Holme-Lacey wasn't the type who had to prove anything.

With his commanding hands on her shoulders again and his mouth invading hers, he eased her down on to the wide double bed. When she was lying in the middle of it, breathless and impatient for him to carry on, he drew back again. Lia felt herself trembling, partly with desire, partly with confusion. She'd been ready for the closeness of his warm, powerful body, and now it was gone she physically ached for it. But Peter seemed in no hurry now, toying with her as she'd toyed with him. He stood by the bed and very slowly began to undress himself.

Lia gave a little smile. There seemed something quaintly old-fashioned about the man removing his own clothes. Normally she did this bit herself. Like a child with her Christmas presents – it was fun unwrapping them when you didn't know what you were going to find. But as she lay there on the bed and watched Peter slowly and deliberately disrobing, she understood. *He* was doing it. *He* was in control.

He'd already kicked off his shoes. Now he was pulling his polo shirt up and over his head. A little thrill went through her at the very first sight of his naked chest. Lia was fascinated by the variety of men's chests – the curve of the pectoral muscles, the differences in body hair. Peter's was trim with absolutely no spare flesh. The scattering of hair wispily covered his stomach, grew thicker over his chest itself and crept up towards his throat. Here and there it seemed to be going grey. But Lia rather liked the novelty of that.

He unzipped his dark trousers. Proper, expensive trousers she noticed, not jeans. Beneath he was wearing silk boxer shorts. She looked for the bulge that would give her a good idea what was in store for her. The petrol-blue silk fell in such a way as to be maddeningly ambiguous. She glimpsed some dark pubic hair through the slit in the front but nothing more before he sank on to the bed beside her.

He isn't hard yet, she thought wryly, and he doesn't want me to see him until he is.

And then all speculation went out of her head. Peter rolled on top of her and his hands were busy with the delicate pearly buttons down the front of her flimsy top. Against the fine material Lia could tell her nipples were peaking hard. She wasn't wearing a bra.

He discovered that soon enough and chuckled in approval. With her helpless beneath him, he began kissing and nuzzling the length of her cleavage. The light cotton top fell completely aside and he moved his oral attention to her erect nipples. He gripped her wrists and pinned them to the bed as he did so. Lia moaned in pleasure and twisted a little. Her movement seemed to spur him on.

'Yes, fight back,' he muttered. 'I love it when women do.'

She strained her arms, pushing back against his weight and the strength of his arms. It was no good. Not only did he have the advantage of greater physical strength, but he was on top, unmoveable. But the act of struggling itself made her own pec muscles contract and her breasts stand prouder. Peter grinned in appreciation at the sight. Then he shifted his position slightly. Through her Indian cotton skirt she felt something warm and hard press against her thigh. Beneath the silk of his boxer shorts was a definite erection.

He rubbed it up and down her thigh. Covered in silk, his cock felt slippery. There was something kinky about the fabric. Something too feminine for a man like Peter Holme-Lacey. For a moment the silk reminded her of Jonathan, but she didn't feel guilty. Jonathan would understand . . .

Peter set her wrists free and began pulling at the elastic waistband of her skirt. Not tugging ineffectually as some men might. This was a long, slow drag that was used to getting what it wanted. Lia flexed her hands for a moment to get the feeling back, and then reached round and felt his buttocks through the silky shorts. The fine, almost translucent material let her feel little curled hairs beneath. The contrast of overt masculinity and decadence intrigued her.

Her skirt was round her thighs now. He eased down her lace panties too, and swept the last of her clothing aside.

Then he stood up again. He was still wearing those boxers but his erection was very obvious now, thrusting out the silk panels in front and leaving a tiny dark spot of moisture in the deep, rich blue. He touched a remote-control panel by the bed and the lights went down.

There was moonlight outside though, and the curtains weren't drawn. It turned everything silver as he knelt on the bed above her and dragged his boxer shorts down. The moonlight gleamed on his hard, high penis. That it was half in shadow made it all the more fascinating – all the more difficult to judge how long or thick it really was.

Lia lay back and spread her thighs. It didn't look like there was any more foreplay on the cards – not that she needed it. Peter just knelt there for a moment, towering over her, the moonlight shining on his naked body, his cock jutting straight out in front of him. That image in itself filled her head with erotic possibilities. His dominance. Her submission.

He'd kept her waiting almost too long. Between her spread thighs her sex was beginning to ache and pulse with unrequited satisfaction. Just as Lia was beginning to writhe and mew in impatience Peter dropped to all fours above her body, grasped her wrists firmly again and then entered her.

For a moment Lia held her breath. This morning she'd felt roughed up after her adventures with the firemen and ready only for Trudi's cunning tongue. For a split second she thought she was going to regret penetrative sex again so soon. But as Peter glided into her she felt only a slight rawness – just a little something to put the edge on sex.

Last night's over-indulgence had made her more sensitive than ever. She felt every millimetre of his cock as it moved within her. That delicious friction. There really was nothing like the feeling of being filled and stretched by a man's bullish erection. And she was hardly going to complain about the good old-fashioned missionary position. The whole length of her vagina tingled with this deep penetration and every time Peter thrust home, the pressure on her clitoris took her one step closer to orgasmic bliss.

But normally she liked to sweep her hands up over a lover's back as he did this to her. Or cup his buttocks and squeeze them in time with his thrusts. Lia wasn't used to being pinned down like this. She tried to free her wrists again but he had them fast. There was no negotiating with his strength. But as she struggled against him, she realised from the grunting change in his breathing that this was turning him on even more.

As he became aroused by her struggles, the speed of his thrusting increased. Lia panicked. She didn't want him to come first. Something told her Peter wasn't a New Man in the bedroom and wouldn't give a damn about her orgasm once he'd had his. She tried to trap his hips between her thighs and slow down his thrusts. She squeezed as hard as she could and almost stopped him in his tracks. Peter roared – in anger, pain or frustration she couldn't work out which. He was trapped, but very deep within her now. Tiny, tiny thrusts were all he could manage and each nudge – so close on the last – against her clitoris brought her closer.

Wrapping her thighs around his buttocks and tensing for all she was worth, she nearly brought him to a standstill. He had to change his stroke. Instead of in and out thrusting he had to writhe his penis inside her like a snake. Lia moaned. This was just the sort of action she'd have used if she was on top – for maximum clitoral pleasure. And the thought of such a man being trapped by her muscular thighs did wild things in her head.

She was ever so close now. The buzzing tightness in her clitoris mounted till it was almost unbearable. Abruptly she released him and let him thrust wildly again – just to feel that furious friction as she tipped over the edge and beautiful waves swept up the sweet core of her body.

Now it was payback time: Peter showed no mercy in his thrusting. He rammed his body into her – but if he only knew how good it felt. Even with the heat from his thrusting, Lia felt the extra warmth and final rush of blood to his cock as he climaxed. And then she was amazed and breathless to feel another warm wave as her vagina blossomed into a second orgasm at that very moment, in sympathy.

For a while afterwards they said nothing. Lia opened her eyes and looked around the room, seeing details she'd understandably missed before. The angle of moonlight had shifted. Now it fell on the foot of the bed. She noticed the footrail had an intricately carved pattern on it. She filed that away for future interest. And the posts at each corner of the bed were carved and chunky. Surely they could have possibilities, too.

Finally Peter had caught his breath enough to whisper, 'I know girls like you. You need something to fight against. Perhaps I realised that before I even met you. We're going to have some fun together, you and I. But I let you off too easy this time. Next time I'll make sure you don't have quite so much room to manoeuvre.'

His muscular arm felt heavy across her waist. The heaviness of possession. Lia felt so restricted she was limited to shallow breaths. By and by she realised Peter wasn't doing this deliberately. His body felt heavy to hers because he was deeply relaxed. Asleep. The deep, unmistakable sleep of a man who'd just had terrific sex.

She eased herself out from under his arm and scrabbled on the floor for her clothes. Peter didn't so much as stir. Lia padded out into the corridor. She was disorientated. It took several false starts down the oak-panelled landings before she found the room the ice-blonde chauffeur had told her was 'hers' for the duration, several hours before.

She clicked on the light. Her things were still in a mess on the single bed and the floor. On impulse she rooted in her rucksack for her mobile phone and checked for messages. There was one text:

Ring me, Jonathan xxx.

Lia glanced at her watch. Ten to twelve. Knowing Jonathan's nocturnal habits he'd only just be getting started.

She made herself comfortable on the narrow bed and dialled his number.

'Hi.'

'Hi back. Been worried about you.'

'Trudi and I can take care of ourselves. But how's Jules? I feel a bit shit about it all.'

'Crashed out on my sofa after drinking me out of schnapps. And mad as hell at you two. I'm keeping my distance.'

'I'm not sure I blame her. Jonathan . . . when she calms down just tell her we still love her to bits and it won't be for long. When the *Lady Jayne* is patched up again things'll be back the way they were.'

'But will they, Lia? Even I can see what's going on. And Jules – well, earlier she was sniffing around a trendy new café bar that's opening up a few streets away. "Vegetable Love" they're calling it.'

'That's wasn't Shakespeare – it was Marvell.'

'Swot. The tourists don't know that.'

There was such a long pause Lia began to wonder if they'd been cut off. Then she heard Jonathan's breathing. She'd always loved the sound of his breathing. Never heavy or coarse, but wispy against her neck in sleep. She missed him.

'What have you been up to?' she asked.

'Generally? Or when you rang?'

'Anytime.'

'When you rang I was lying in bed thinking about you. I found some stuff you left one time. I think it was you anyway. I put it on.'

Lia mentally flicked through a roll call of her possessions. What was missing? With most of her stuff still on the beleaguered *Lady Jayne* it was difficult to tell. And knowing Jonathan, he could be talking about anything from perfume to nail varnish to a full basque and stockings set.

'What are you wearing?'

'That pearl choker. Three lines of pearls. It is yours, isn't it?'

'Fortunately for you, yes.'

She imagined it. There was something about the thought of Jonathan in pearls. On another sort of man – Denny or Peter, for instance – the effect would have been utterly ridiculous. But Jonathan – fine boned and with his long, dark, silky hair – was sexually ambiguous enough to carry it off, even look attractive in a kinky kind of way.

'Anything else?' She rather liked the idea of Jonathan naked apart from her pearls. The way they would gleam against the fine, dark hair in the little hollow at the base of his throat. She imagined herself running her fingertips over the pearls' bumpy warm-from-his-body texture, and then carrying on to sweep her palms down over his soft chest hair and yielding belly. A glow of desire began to rise in her again. She cradled the phone in one hand, lay back a little more and burrowed a hand up under her skirt to finger her moist labia.

'Actually there is,' he replied. 'A cream-coloured camisole. With lace on the neckline. Deep lace. Bit of a tight fit, but I kind of like it. I like the way it presses against my nipples.'

Lia slipped a finger inside her warm sex as she thought about it. Jonathan had sensitive, almost feminine nipples. And she knew from past experience that the feeling of a fine silk camisole being stretched across her own pouting nipples and then having them tongued through the silk was mind-blowing.

'I wish I was there to lick them for you.'

'I'll rub them. We can pretend you're doing it.'

'You wearing anything else of mine?'

'Those stretch lace panties that match the camisole.'

'Mmm. I can just imagine. Your cock must be a really tight fit inside them. If you're hard, that is. I assume you're hard.'

'I am now. And the lace is so tight it feels kinda scratchy against me. But it's good. I feel all bound up.'

'Are you rubbing yourself through the lace?'

'I'm stroking the outside of your panties. It's driving me crazy. What d'you reckon I should do?'

'I reckon you should hook your cock out. Give him room to enjoy himself.'

'But he's enjoying himself right now. And the feel of the lace pressing him right up against me is fantastic. I'm just going to stroke him. Tease him. This is going to take a long time . . .'

'God, I wish I was there with you. I'd kiss you all up and down the length of your cock through the lace. I'd run the tip of my nose all over your groin.' Lia paused for a moment, inhaled and imagined she was taking in the nostril-tightening scent of Jonathan's pheromones. 'Then I'd peel the lace down. I wouldn't be able to help myself. I'd take the end of your cock in my mouth and suck and suck until you came.'

'Wouldn't be long. Won't be, I mean. Forget what I said about teasing and taking my time. I really want to rub my cock hard now. I'm so horny I'll go crazy if I don't. I'm slipping your panties off. I'm using them in my hand. I'm rubbing myself with them. Oh Lia, it's an amazing way to have a wank. I feel I'm really doing it to you.'

She lay back fully and tucked the phone into the crook of her shoulder. Both hands were free now. She burrowed the left one under her skimpy top and squeezed her bra-less nipples tight. She needed such extreme stimulation. Jonathan might well be on the point of coming. She didn't want him to leave her behind.

'I wish I was there with you,' she breathed and she really, really meant it. Times like this, with Jonathan, reminded her what was special about him. He was her playmate. Sex was fun with him – an adventure, playful, creative, free. Her mind could soar with his to outrageous places. Sex with him was truly in the head as well as in the loins.

'If I was there with you,' she continued, 'I'd do everything. I'd cover every inch of your beautiful, kinky body with nibbles and kisses. I'd lick your cock and twirl my tongue into the little eye of your foreskin and lap up all that saltiness. And when your erection was trembling and straining, I'd rear up and impale myself on you, sucking you deep into the very centre of my body – all red and warm and soft and where I know you'd like to be.'

Here, Lia thrust her fingers as deep into her own pussy as far as they'd go. She was close now. But she genuinely longed for her busy fingers to be Jonathan's cock.

'I'd suck your tits as you dangled them in my face.' As Jonathan said it, Lia pinched her nipples just that little bit harder. 'Because I know that turns you on. You'd be riding me so rough they'd keep jumping away from me – as you bounced about – but the sight of them wobbling – would make the blood pump so hard into my cock that – yes!'

There was a sharp cry on the other end of the line and Lia knew he'd climaxed, probably soaking her lacy panties with his come. She rammed her fingers home into her tender sex and pressed the heel of her hand fiercely against her mons, hitting the trigger spot on her clitoris and joining him in sweet, violent orgasm.

When she picked up the phone properly again the line had gone dead. Had one or other of them hit the wrong button in their excitement? Surely he wouldn't deliberately have hung up. With Jonathan, that post-orgasmic intimacy was very genuine. She felt cheated.

She lay there for a few moments, on the point of sleep to sated to move. She only snatched her hand out of her panties and sat up again when she heard a deliberate footfall in the corridor outside.

Peter Holme-Lacey opened her door without knocking.

'So this is where you got to. No need to be coy. Come back to bed. I've got an early start to get to Birmingham International tomorrow morning but there's no reason why we can't make the most of having to get up early . . .'

He tightened his hand round her bicep. It was that grip again – the one that didn't hurt but Lia knew full well could – if he wanted it to.

'You know I'll look after you,' he continued and she knew he would. On his terms.

The mobile still in her other hand warbled as a text came through. She glanced at it quickly, turning the display aside slightly so Peter couldn't read it:

Love you. Jonathan xxxx
Damn.

CHAPTER

7

L ia slid the tray of vol-au-vents out of the oven and breathed in deeply. The flaky pastry had that cooked-to-perfection buttery aroma. Now she had this whole huge kitchen to play with there was no need to fall back on the frozen stuff.

The weather had cooled over the past couple of days. It was overcast, a chilly breeze was rattling the flaps of the extractor fan and she actually felt grateful for the warmth of the full size commercial ovens. In fact, the kitchen felt warm all over. A safe place to be. One that didn't rock, one where you didn't bump your elbow against your mate's head as you reached for the Thousand Island dressing. Lia couldn't remember feeling this protected.

Trudi burst in, banging the door back on its hinges. 'Glorified bloody waitresses, that's what we are.' She picked up another tray of canapés from the large, scrubbed central tables.

'Don't be so overdramatic. We planned this whole menu, didn't we? That's as creative as anything we ever did on the boat.'

'You going soft or what?' Trudi's lip curled. 'Tell you what, though. That delegate from the regional tourist board is all right. Caught him looking where he shouldn't have been a few times.'

Balancing her tray, Trudi smoothed her black skirt down over her thighs with one hand as she said this. Peter Holme-Lacey had provided them with 'appropriate' uniforms of smart white blouses and black skirts that were supposed to come just above the knee. With Trudi's extra height hers ended mid-thigh. Lia wasn't surprised men looked.

'He's wearing a wedding ring.'

'Ah, so you've noticed him too. Seriously, Li, get out there and let me take a turn in the kitchen.' She winked. 'A bit of harmless flirting keeps the pulse going.'

'I'm fine as I am.'

'What's the matter? Boss man doesn't like you putting it about? Oh don't look at me like that, Li. You might not have seen fit to tell me all the graphic details but I've known you long enough to know when you're doing it with someone.'

Trudi swept out again. Lia felt stung. It was true – she hadn't brought up the subject of her relationship with Peter. The time had never seemed right. Did Trudi feel shut out by that? Was it another nail in the coffin of the 'all for one and one for all' mateyness the three of them once shared?

And that wasn't the only thing they shared that had gone down the drain. They'd been here a week or so now and neither of them had alluded to the intimacy that had been shattered that morning in the firemen's house. Their unfinished business. Did Trudi feel she'd made a mistake and wanted to put it behind her? Or had the free-loving spark gone out of them both? Lia noticed Trudi had tried flirting once or twice with Peter's glacial, androgynous chauffeur, whom they'd since learned was called Marlene. She'd felt a prickle, though she wasn't quite sure if she'd label it jealousy. Not that Trudi had got any more than a cool look for her overtures.

The swing door clunked open again.

'Back so soon?' Lia said without looking up. 'And what's on offer from the tourist board? Oh, sorry. Wasn't expecting you.'

Marlene herself was standing there. Her face was an impassive, too-perfect mask. Lia had never quite worked out what her role was in this set up. She was more than just a chauffeur. Since Peter had left for his latest set of meetings in Prague, Lia got the distinct impression Marlene was keeping an eye on them in his absence. She doubted Peter had any real sexual interest in the tall Teutonic iceberg; he probably just found the frisson of keeping a beautiful, if ambivalent, female chauffeur amusing.

'I'm going now,' Marlene announced in her clipped way. 'The Boss phoned half an hour ago.' She always called him 'The Boss'. At first Lia had wondered – half flippantly, half resentfully – if it indicated some domination scene going on between them. But she soon decided it was just her way of speaking. 'I'm meeting him at the airport. But he has some business to attend to en route. We'll be back this evening.'

'Okay. Oh, could you do me a favour before you go? You wouldn't happen to have a swimsuit I could borrow? I really fancy a dip after we've finished with this lot and most of my stuff's still marooned on board the *Lady Jayne*.'

'Swimming in the river? Don't be foolish.'

'I actually had the pool in mind.'

'He's very possessive about that. Not just anyone is allowed to use it.' Marlene raised one finely plucked eyebrow. 'But maybe you are a special case. I'll see what I can do.'

She turned without a goodbye. Lia shrugged. Perhaps despite her odd manner Marlene wasn't so bad.

When the conference delegates had gone back in for their last session Trudi said to her, 'Right, that's us free for another few days. Who've we got lined up next?'

'Some bird conservation charity's AGM, I think.'

'Ah, Greenies. Jules's veggie samosas could have come in handy after all. You heard anything about how she's doing?'

'I've had a few texts from Jonathan.' The memory brought a smile back to Lia's face. Most of the texts had been positively depraved but she hadn't quite had the heart to answer them yet. 'Apparently Jules is still calling us all the names under the sun and is developing an interest in Jonathan's old hacking routines. I just hope she comes back in with us when the *Lady Jayne*'s ready to go again.'

'And when's that going to be? If Holme-Lacey's back tonight you need to pin him down on that one.'

'He's been out of the country for days. One elderly narrowboat will be the last thing on his mind.'

'You're making excuses. I was right – you are

going soft on him.' But she winked and squeezed Lia's elbow to take the sting out of her voice. Afterwards Lia realised it was probably the first time Trudi had touched her for ages.

When she went back up to her room she found a swimsuit hanging by its shoulder strap on her doorhandle. It wasn't the sexiest piece of swimwear she'd ever seen. Plain dark blue and a thick texture – a little like the kind of fabric wetsuits are made from. It had a high neckline and a zip that came part way down the front. Lia turned it over dubiously in her hands. She knew what Trudi would have said: to hell with swimsuits, go skinny dipping. But she wasn't quite Trudi. Also the swimming pool was housed in that big conservatory, and you could never be quite sure who was going to turn up at the Holme-Lacey residence.

So Lia took it into her room and tried it on. It was too tight over the bust – not surprising, given Marlene's more boyish figure. The whole thing just about fitted if she undid the front zip, though. Lia turned this way and that in the mirror to check the effect. Well, it certainly gave her one hell of a cleavage.

She grabbed a large, white towel, wrapped it sarong-like about her and bare-footed it down to the pool. All the conference delegates had long gone now and the house seemed very quiet.

Part of her had been worried that the door to the annexe might have been locked. Peter could be like that sometimes. But it clicked open smoothly. She found the switch on the side wall that illuminated the pool from underneath. The blue water was perfectly still and glassy. Everything was silent. It

110

seemed a magical place.

Lia dropped her towel on the side and plunged in. All this space to herself! The sheer childish glee of being the first person to break the water's mirror-flat surface, like being the first one to leave footprints in virgin snow or to stab a spoon through the foil on a new jar of coffee. All about being first. Asserting your ownership. She could understand how the feeling went to Peter's head.

She turned in the water, revelling in the way it streamed off her body, caressing it. Normally in a public swimming pool she never would have had the time or mental space to fully appreciate how sensual the caress of water could be. She did back-stroke up and down for several lengths. Lia loved backstroke. Just doing it without fear of bumping into anyone felt like an indulgence. And right now she could glide on her back and look up not at municipal tiles and strip lights but at the evening sky darkening beyond the conservatory's high glass roof.

After another few lazy, rhythmic lengths she paused for breath, half hauling herself out against the side. That was when she noticed the white metal spiral staircase in one corner of the annexe. It led to a door high up in the original house wall. Thinking for a few moments about the mansion's geography, Lia realised it must come out very close to Peter's bedroom.

Maybe he came down for an early-morning swim – when he wasn't with her. She knew nothing about his routine. There was a lot about Peter she didn't know – and he didn't seem to want her to know. It made him infuriating and intriguing. But his mature body was so toned and firm and inviting for her to run her hands across. Early morning swimming seemed to fit the bill.

Once she'd caught her breath Lia turned and launched into the water again. This time she did breaststroke. The description became very literally true. With the unzipped front of her too-tight swimsuit gaping open, little eddies of water funnelled down her cleavage, tickling. Lia grinned in pleasure. Her sensuous instincts, never far below the surface, were rising warmly again. What time was Peter due home? Had Marlene even said? Or, if not Peter, had Trudi seemed more open this afternoon or was that just wishful thinking?

She became bored with proper swimming and just let her body play as it wanted to in the water. She rolled over and over like a seal, enjoying the physical pressure of the water on her body. She held her breath and dived to the bottom, her loose hair billowing out like a warm brown cloud about her.

Finally she leaned backwards on to the side and let her legs kick up choppy little waves. She rejoiced in the smoothness of her skin slicing through the water. Her legs' absolute hairlessness meant she felt physical sensations with an intensity that turned them into two long, active sensuous zones.

Peter liked his women depilated smooth and smothered in body lotion. She'd become almost fanatical about it over the past week. And she'd never adapted herself to a man's tastes before. They'd all had to take her as they found her – the free-spirit that Denny and Jonathan had fallen for. What was happening to her? She felt as if she was surrendering – not just to his fierce, dominant love-making but his intellect, too. She knew surrender was dangerous. But danger had a certain spice about it.

Half reclining against the edge of the pool, lost in the churning of the waves she was making and the splashing that filled her head, Lia didn't hear the subtle click of the far door opening.

Suddenly she realised that Peter was standing at the poolside, looking down at her. He had something long and dark in his hands she didn't recognise at first. He was casually dressed – not as if he'd just come from a business meeting – and his dark hair was slightly damp.

Lia froze. But the waves carried on lapping around her, accusing her of having trespassed in his private pool. Peter was looking at her in a way she couldn't read. But he was good at that. More than once since being here she'd felt like he was the older man in some classic novel and she was the young wife who came in to the big, mysterious house and was expected to miraculously know all the rules.

Eventually she said, 'You didn't tell me I wasn't supposed to.'

'Clearly not.' Then he grinned. 'I was just about to hang this up somewhere to dry.' He raised the thing he was holding and she recognised it at last: a diver's wetsuit. 'But perhaps I'd do better to follow your example. Don't go running off, now.'

He slipped into a cubicle at the foot of the spiral staircase. Why the coyness? Lia wondered. She'd seen him naked often enough. But Peter liked to stay in control. He was teasing her. Making her go at his pace.

When he emerged again he was wearing the wetsuit. Lia giggled. She'd never seen someone wearing one up close before and had only thought about them in a nudge-nudge, smirk sort of way. The suit certainly took no prisoners. On a lesser physique it would have given away every surplus ripple of flesh. It fitted Peter perfectly. She could make out the curve of his pectoral muscles and the hollowness of his hard belly. But not as clearly as if he'd been naked. The texture of the suit itself was a tease, leaving half the work tantalisingly to her memory and imagination.

Peter dived into the pool with a loud splash. He ploughed the half length towards her in a noisy, expansive crawl, scattering water droplets across the surface. Making his mark, as he always did.

'Well, my mermaid,' he said as surfaced in front of her. 'I've found you fishing in the forbidden pool. What should I do with you?'

'Take me prisoner?'

'I think I may have to do that.'

He pinned her up against the side of the pool, crushing his body against hers as he kissed her. As his tongue snaked into her mouth he began rubbing and grinding their bodies together. The roughened texture of his wet suit and her costume made a strange scratching noise. It was hardly sexy in the same way whispering silk was sexy but there was something edgier about it. Something a little on the wilder side.

'Why this?' she asked, wriggling away from him a moment before her rising desire grew too heated: God, she *had* missed him. She really had.

'I've been diving. Stopped on my way back. Joined the group that was inspecting your handi-work on the *Lady Jayne*.' He paused just long enough for her to feel slapped down by that. It was never far away: the knowledge that she was here because she'd got too cocky and their treasured boat had paid the price. 'Don't worry. The damage really is only superficial. But the state of your engine – the boatyard were amazed it kept you going so long. Now, let's think about more interesting matters. Does this zip come down any further? No? Ah well, I can see plenty as it is . . .'

He slipped a couple of fingers into her cleavage and began to stroke. The water trickling between her breasts had fanned a rising glow of need already. Now the more assertive pressure of his touch meant the need was something she couldn't ignore.

In turn she began to caress his body. The zip of his own wetsuit was already slipping down a little. His crinkly chest hair peeped out over the top of it. She loved that – when men's body hair escaped just a little from their clothes, it was like a glimpse of a promise just waiting for the right moment to be fulfilled.

Lia caught the tag of his zip and began to ease it down, exposing more dark chest hair as she did. It wasn't easy to concentrate as he was still stroking the responsive upper curves of her breasts. His touch made her more and more impatient. Ripples of need fanned up through her body. She felt acutely the pressure of her tight swimsuit and longed for him to strip it off her.

She'd eased his zip all the way down to his navel by now.

'D'you think I put this on purely so you could have the pleasure of taking it off a few minutes later?' he asked. She nodded. 'Well . . . you're absolutely right.'

Peter did the rest himself, shrugging the wet suit off his well-squared, masculine shoulders and peeling it down his thighs. Lia was piqued: he still never let her undress him. It had to be on his terms.

He let the wet suit float in the water beside them and pressed his body close to hers again. She could feel his cock against her thigh – interested but not fully erect. Surely the water wasn't that cold? Maybe he just needed a little more motivation after what must have been several long days.

He bent his head to hers and played around a moment, dancing his lips across hers, teasingly, before he kissed her. The pressure of his hands on her shoulders kept her from rising in the water to meet him. He sensed her need. He played on it. He kept her wanting. His lips nipped and glanced over her upturned face, his lightly stubbled cheeks grazed hers. The scent of expensive, spicy after-shave liberated by the little splashes of water tickled her nose. Lia didn't normally go for aftershave, but this one was different. She'd never smelt it before. Classy. She drew it deep into her lungs and held it there. A scent that had become hot-wired in her brain and associated purely with him.

As he pressed his lips more forcefully on to hers, he invaded her with his thick, mobile tongue. She let him invade. Just for a moment. She was just going to fool him into thinking she'd surrendered. But the feeling was so sweet. Any second now she was surely going to break away and make him work for it – but Lia let the seconds tick by while his overwhelming, naked masculinity pressed her against the side of the pool.

His hands began moving in circles on her shoulders. Slowly they slid down the straps of her restrictive swimsuit. Her breasts bobbed free into the water. It was such a sweet relief not to be bound by the thick, unyielding fabric. It was an even sweeter relief when Peter cupped her breasts in his big, capable hands and began rasping the pads of his thumbs over her nipples. Exposure to the air had already tightened them into high, hard buds and they were super sensitive under the pressure of his thumbs. Peter began tracing the edges of both thumbnails over her areolae and from time to time even grazed them over the very tips of her nipples themselves. It was a tiny, subtle movement. A caress that stopped just short of pain. Lia tipped her head back, avoiding the distraction of his possessive tongue now. She just wanted to concentrate on what he was doing to her nipples. It felt so intense.

And it turned him on too – she could feel his hard cock jousting with her thighs now. But he hadn't slipped the swimsuit down any further than her midriff and her pounding sex was still encased in that restrictive stuff she'd come to hate. She so longed to feel his hot erection nudging open her welcoming lips.

'Undress me, Peter,' she gasped. 'All the way down. I'm so horny for your cock.'

He chuckled in her ear. She could just melt at the rich, brown sugar-and-all-things-bad sound of that low, wicked laugh. It was mature and decadent and spoke of years of experience she had yet to acquire. And it was a power thing, too.

'You young girls,' he murmured, 'how will I ever keep up with you? And have you ever thought what a logistical nightmare it is doing it in a swimming pool?'

Lia hadn't. She'd been too carried away with the

feeling and the longing to be penetrated again.
There was that time in the bath with Denny, of
course. They'd knelt up, clear of the water and that
had been fantastic. But here . . . ?

'There are ways,' she whispered back. 'Maybe
you just need someone to teach you to be creative.'

'What makes you think you can teach me
anything, little girl?'

But all the same, he was tugging down her
swimsuit. He eased it over her thighs and cupped
her silky soft buttocks for a moment. She'd been
keeping her skin smooth and anointed for him.
Just the way he liked it. And she was proud of the
response she got as he fondled her arse – a low
moan of appreciation.

She stepped out of the swimsuit and let it float
away on the surface of the water. They were both
completely naked now. He kissed her again,
moulding the whole front of his bare body against
hers. She ground her soft chest against the hairiness of his, the obvious contrast so sweet, the
subtle stimulation of his chest hairs on her skin so
delicious. Under the water his cock swayed and
swam between her legs. She clasped her thighs
tight, making him her prisoner.

'You still want it here and now, little girl? You
want me to thrust this up your sweet little pussy?'

'You said I was a mermaid when you got in.
Maybe I haven't got one. Maybe I'm inviolable.'

'No one's that perfect. Maybe mermaids are
simply virginal and I'll just have to do a little opening. But anyway, my mermaid. I have other plans
for you tonight.'

A devilish flash rose in her. Peter was teasing
her again. Making her wait – making her play by

his rules. Or, what had he said on that very first night they'd talked? About not winning too easily. About it spoiling the fun. Was he goading her into something?

Whether she was being manipulated or not, Lia seized the opportunity. Peter had relaxed his hold on her buttocks. She twisted away from him and kicked off against the side, pushing herself far out into the pool.

'Whatever your plans are, you'll have to catch me first.'

Peter was a good swimmer. She'd worked that one out. But he hadn't seen her in action before and she could tell he was surprised at how good she was. And she had youth and suppleness on her side. And something else, too. In the days he'd been away she'd been pampering herself with all the rich cocoa butter lotions he'd left for her, and a little residue was left on the surface of her skin. Every time he grasped for her arm or her calf, she slipped, fish-like, away from him.

The smile began to fade from Peter's eyes as she spun away in the water yet another time, sending up a rising curtain of droplets with her skimming hands. He liked the chase, but Peter Holme-Lacey chased to win. Doubt was creeping into his pale blue eyes.

Lia gasped in a deep breath and dived beneath him. She touched the bottom of the pool as she evaded his scrabbling fingertips. Opening her eyes she could see his body above hers in the water but everything was fuzzy. She couldn't tell if he still had an erection with the tension of the game or whether his immediate randiness was fading.

As she surfaced again her back brushed against

his flank. He made a final grab for her long, loose hair but she flipped over again like a seal breaching the water and made a fast front crawl for the side.

He was seconds behind her as she mounted the poolside steps and she felt the snapping movement of air as his hand closed on the space where her ankle had just been. She grabbed the big fluffy towel – losing a precious moment or so – and, wrapping it round her, headed for the white spiral steps at the far end of the annexe.

She was younger and fitter than Peter and, glancing back, she realised it probably wasn't easy to run with such an erection. She gained a few seconds on the stairs. And then she wondered whether he was letting her get away. Whether he knew something she didn't. The whole thing had been a spontaneous bit of fun as far as she'd been concerned so she hadn't stopped to think of this before. But was the door at the top locked?

Lia collapsed against the panelled door. She was breathing heavily and very aware of the water dripping from her hair and down her back. It wasn't that she didn't want to be caught. Whatever Peter did to her when he'd 'won' promised to be exciting. But the childish part of her wanted to spin out the game. She wanted to 'win' too.

She tried the curvy wrought-iron handle. The door wouldn't budge.

Peter's footfalls on the steps behind her became slower as he realised she was trapped. Lia turned and looked. He hadn't bothered with a towel and the water was still running off his impressively toned body. Although there were a few goose bumps here and there on his damp skin it didn't spoil his composure. Her gaze was drawn down irresistibly to his wet, crinkled pubic hair and his penis rearing sturdily above it. No mistaking – Peter enjoyed the game he'd won.

'I've always had a problem with that door sticking,' he murmured. 'Should have complained to the people who installed it before now, I suppose. Never got round to it. You have to lift the handle just a fraction and pull it towards you, just so, before you push it down. See? It's a knack, like so many things in life. And how convenient. You did realise we were just down the corridor from my room . . . ?'

He laid a hand on Lia's hip, swaddled in its thick towel, and steered her in the direction he wanted her to go.

Once inside his room he turned the lights to dim and pulled the towel from around her breasts. They dried each other on it, even wrapping themselves up in it at the same time: a child-like den away from the rest of the world. There must have been other towels in the en suite bathroom, but sharing this was special. He took the last dry corner and dabbed her face. There could be such tenderness, Lia realised, even in surrender.

But . . . this isn't Peter's usual style, she thought. It's more like Jonathan's. What's he up to?

'Stand at the foot of the bed,' he told her when they were both dry. 'I know you've been eyeing it up. I think you'll find it's just the right height for you.'

She did as she was told. The carved wood was level with her bush. She pressed her mons against it and rolled her hips experimentally. There was enough diffuse pleasure reaching her clit to make this interesting.

Peter came and stood behind her. She could feel his hard-on pressing into the cleft of her arse. Now they were both dry his erection felt hotter than ever. Hot and ready for action. And she wouldn't need much foreplay. The whole business in the swimming pool had been foreplay of a kind. The thrill of their chasing game had her pussy glowing in readiness.

He reached round and began running his hands up and down her belly between her navel and the very top of her bush. It wasn't the most immediately obvious erogenous zone. But she soon found his caress drew a very deep sensuous response from her. It was as if he were arousing her very womb, calling to her femininity on a profound, primitive level. One thing she knew: the slow-burning feelings he provoked in her weren't going to fade for a long, long time.

'Now,' Peter whispered in her ear in between kissing the side of her neck, 'the trouble with you, little girl, is I never know when you're going to run off on me. Wouldn't it be a tragedy if we both got ourselves worked up into a frenzy and you decided to play another of your little games? I'm going to have to find a way of keeping you here.'

She felt his warmth move away from her for a moment and heard the sound of a drawer opening. When he snuggled up close behind her again she glanced down and saw he had some soft leather straps in his hands.

She'd played bondage games before with Jonathan. It didn't faze her. Though usually he was the one who wanted to be tied up. And the accent had been on 'play'. With Peter ... well, she wondered.

'Keep your hands on that rail,' he murmured. 'Lean forward just a fraction. There. It's conveniently designed, don't you think? Now, the straps are soft. So soft. Nothing to be afraid of . . .'

He wound the leather round her wrists – firmly but not too tight. When he'd finished there was no room to move in the straps, but it didn't hurt. And to keep her balance she had to thrust her butt assertively towards him.

Peter chuckled that throaty chuckle she loved so much and reached round again to cup her breasts.

'You feel fantastic at this angle,' he told her. 'Gives them that extra bit more weight. And you're so vulnerable trussed up like that. I can help myself to what I want, anytime I want. Reminds me of those buxom ladies they used to carve on the prows of ships. You ever thought of having something like that on the *Lady Jayne*?' He went quiet for a moment, moulding her breasts more vigorously and clearly going off into a pleasant fantasy of his own. 'No, perhaps not. Wouldn't go with the corporate image. While you and your friends might like an unconventional life, we professional types like to keep our fantasies safe behind the bedroom door. And you're in my world now, little girl. You play by my rules.'

He was tweaking her nipples hard now. A little high-pitched moan escaped Lia's throat. She wanted him to penetrate her. She knew he was ready: she could feel the heat of his cock against her thrust-out bottom. Why was he waiting?

'Something we were saying earlier, my mermaid.' He began to rearrange the still-damp trails of her hair on the back of her neck even as he whispered to her. 'About mermaids being virginal.

Inviolable. Something tells me there's a place you are still a virgin. I think it's appropriate that an experienced, older man should be the first to penetrate you there.'

He parted her tight buttocks and began running the tip of his cock up and down the secret cleft between. Lia tensed against her leather bonds. It was an automatic reaction. Nothing to be scared of, she told herself. Plenty of people do it. Trudi's done it loads. Why the hell didn't I ever think to ask her for advice . . . ?

'You've guessed?' he breathed softly in her ear. 'I'm going to enjoy this. I'm going to enjoy fucking your so-tight arse, little girl. But first . . . I wouldn't want you to accuse me of not being gentle.'

He moved away from her again and she heard a drawer slide in and out. Then she smelled a scent she recognised. The rich, almost sinfully chocolatey scent of the cocoa butter lotion he liked to smell all over her. He'd poured a generous palmful. Now he was rubbing it into the cleft of her arse.

He concentrated on the sensitive ring of her anus. She relaxed and let him slip a finger inside. Once she'd got over the taboo, she realised how sensual it felt. How naughty. How full of tiny, tingling nerve endings that entrance to her body was. As she relaxed even more and he slipped two fingers inside, she found out just how sexy it could be.

Lia had always thought women 'gave in' to anal sex. That it was a one-sided thing because men liked to feel a tighter hole enveloping their pricks. She hadn't bargained with it feeling so good. Revelling in the forbiddeness of it. All these years she'd been missing out on this sensitive playground.

As he slipped two fingers deeply into her, right up to the knuckle, Lia gave out a low, involuntary moan. Peter withdrew his fingers and went in with his cock.

She braced herself for his normal bullish thrusting. But this was different. Peter was very controlled. He barely moved within her tighter passage – perhaps his needs were different here? The slippery, rich body lotion oozing in and out of her gave everything an erotically slithery feel. She loved his tiny movements. She felt every precise stroke inside.

It was eerie – the feeling of being over-full and penetrated, yet not penetrated at the same time. She clenched her buttocks against him and ground her pubis fiercely into the carved wooden swirl at the foot of the bed. Yes, this was perfect. She could definitely up the pitch of her arousal this way.

Then Peter reached round to fondle her breasts again. His hands smelled richly of cocoa butter and something else – her own scent, naughty and erotic but nothing to be ashamed of. He covered her breasts with that same scent as he cupped and squeezed them. Lia relaxed and gave herself over to the voluptuous, if novel, sexy sensations that were taking over her body.

Peter's cock was moving more vigorously now. It was as if he were fighting against his need to thrust for all he was worth. Lia pressed her mons against the wooden rail and filled her head with wild thoughts. She was feeling a little raw now. She held on to the notion of being split, opened, burst apart by Peter's prick. As a fantasy, it packed a punch. She was beginning to feel she could come this way.

She shifted the angle of her hips a little. It favoured the pressure of her clitoris against the bed. But it seemed to be a difficult angle for Peter. He grunted in frustration and his thrusts slowed again to almost a static grind and roll. She felt she was closer than he was. She filled her head with the dirty thoughts of his cock filling up her arse and then she climaxed. Her orgasm swept up through her and this time the warm, sweet spasm seemed to take in her invaded back passage too. A completely new feeling. One she wouldn't be without.

Lia took pity on him. After all, he was the master who had brought her to this unexpected sexual pleasure. She poked her bottom out in his direction again and let him thrust as much as he needed to. The feeling was becoming more than raw. It was fiery. But she was enjoying the fire.

When he came she could feel him swell and burst every bit as intensely as if he'd climaxed in her vagina. Perhaps more so.

For a while she kept her muscles tensed against letting him go. That was something else superbly under her control with anal penetration. But finally she did let him withdraw. He untied her leather bonds and rubbed the feeling back tenderly into her forearms.

'I'm glad to have been the first man to do that to you.'

'I wish I'd known what I was missing. I'd have tried it years ago.'

'No. You had to wait to meet the right man. That was me. An older man needs to initiate you.'

He sat down on the bed and drew her down

beside him. 'Don't fight me, Lia. And don't double cross me. Don't even think about it. We have something private. Remember where you're safe.'

He lay back without even bothering to pull the sheet over him. She lay down beside him but her head was too full and buzzing to let her sleep. True, they'd shared something so very intimate. But again he was trying to make a take-over bid for everything inside her head.

Peter's breathing had fallen into its rhythmic sleeping pattern. Lia felt too hot and sticky to be this close. She retrieved the towel from the floor, wrapped it round her and tiptoed back to her own room. This time she didn't lose her way.

A few moments after she'd got into bed there was a soft tap at the door and a feminine whisper. 'Li, I thought I heard you come back. You there?'

Trudi came in, sat down on her bed and patted her duvet-covered legs – just in a sisterly sort of way.

Lia hauled herself sleepily up on one elbow. 'Just in case you thought I was slacking – I got something out of Peter about the *Lady Jayne*. He inspected her this afternoon. The crash damage wasn't too bad but apparently our engine was living on borrowed time.'

'Hmm, so we're no nearer getting away from this place? I tell you, Li, it gives me the creeps. Like a set for "The Addams Family" or something. But I've got something to tell you, too. I had a long chat on the phone with Jules this evening.'

'Oh? Who rang who?'

'She rang me, believe it or not. Do you want the good news, the bad news or the possibly brilliant news?'

'As it comes.'

'Well, the good news is at least she's talking to us again. The bad news is she's wangled herself a job at that new veggie restaurant round the corner from Jonathan's. Though perhaps that's what's put her in a better mood. It may be temporary but she was disturbingly cagey about that. And the possibly brilliant news is that she's had this idea. Only, you need to do your fifth columnist bit again.' She winked and patted Lia's thigh. 'But I know how you enjoy that.'

CHAPTER

8

———

'You never bring me presents back from your travels,' Lia murmured, reaching over in bed and twirling the hairs on Peter's bare chest. 'Where was it this time? Brussels again?'

She knew perfectly well where it had been. Though Peter's itinerary of international business meetings had been as cosmopolitan as ever these past two weeks, she'd kept tabs on his comings and goings. She'd made it her business to.

'Yes it was Brussels. So what?'

'Isn't that supposed to be the lace capital of Europe? So by my reckoning you owe me something lacy. I can't believe your meetings don't leave you time to visit a few tasteful lingerie shops.'

'What's this – are you turning into a high maintenance woman on me?'

They both grinned. He liked her like this. She knew it. He liked her being uppity and demanding so he could have the satisfaction of believing he kept her in check. What he didn't realise was how good an actress she was. And how close he was to rising to the bait.

'Anyway,' Lia continued, 'just think how much you'd like me in something lacy. Imagine it.'

'I've got a wicked imagination.'

'I know. Even better. So how about it?'

She rolled over so she was half on his chest and pressed her bare breasts against him. The warmth of his body seeped into hers. It felt delicious. It really wasn't an act. If she could forget for a moment that he was a hopeless control freak who meddled in their business and didn't trust her two best friends, the simple fact of being with Peter on a warm, lazy morning like this was pure physical pleasure.

'I'll bring you something back from Amsterdam. I should be able to find something naughty enough there, even for you.'

'But you're not due to go till the week after next.'

'When did I appoint you as my PA?'

He was smiling. But his eyes were narrowed as if an edge of suspicion had crept in. She'd rattled off his itinerary too fast, she realised. One thing control freaks hate is other people getting a handle on them. Peter was so compulsively secret he had all his records on one system and only reluctantly let his real PA have access to it.

Lia moved her body against his. Distraction time. And it was distracting her, too. Her breasts swung freely and her nipples grazed the springy hairs on his chest. The sleeping glow of desire began to wake and snake its way up inside her. And as she felt something rise and harden against her bare thigh the temptation just to mount him, ride him and forget all about subterfuge was nearly killing her.

'What I mean is,' she said between kisses, 'I'll have to wait too long for that. I'm impatient. I want my present now.'

'Little girl. Where am I going to get you a present this far out in the country and at half past six on a Sunday morning?'

Bait, bait. She was laying it carefully for him.

'You're on-line. Connecting to the Internet should be a breeze this time in the morning.'

'Good point. You can help me choose, then. Afterwards . . .'

He cupped her buttocks and tried to guide her hips up and fully on to his. He clearly wanted what had been going through her mind. And it was hard to refuse. The empty ache of longing filled her vagina and, besides, Lia really did love being on top. It would have been the easiest thing in the world to listen to that ache.

'Now who's impatient?' She kissed her way over his neck and whispered in his ear. 'Let's go have a look at a few sites. It'll be fun. It'll get us both going.'

'I already am. And unless I'm very much mistaken . . .' He slipped a hand down between her legs and fingered her moistening pussy. I wish you wouldn't, Lia thought. You could so easily convince me . . .

'Ever heard of delayed gratification?' She gasped involuntarily as he slipped a finger inside her. She was horny enough now that it almost hurt. And to have such a virile, ready man a prisoner beneath her made it so very, very easy to forget she had a job to do. 'Come on. Let's go look at some naughty websites.'

She rolled off him abruptly before she had time to change her mind. The look Peter gave her was difficult to read. His eyes were narrowed again. Was he riled he hadn't got his way? Or intrigued by her suggestion?

'You win,' he grunted. 'And if you must know, I've bookmarked all the best lingerie sites . . .'

She doubted he knew any more than she did. Surfing all the sex-toy sites just for a laugh had often been a favourite late-night game between her and Jonathan. Sometimes he'd hack in and leave childish comments like, 'Jonathan really recommends this because . . .' The prospect of doing something with Peter that she'd done before with him left a tight feeling just under her solar plexus. It made Jonathan feel closer. But at the same time she felt disloyal. She hadn't texted him for weeks, now.

Peter was already out of bed. She caught a flash of his erection fading a little before he wrapped his dark silk dressing gown around himself. 'Come on. What are you waiting for?'

Lia swung out of bed and pulled on one of Peter's discarded T-shirts. It barely covered her butt. She'd always liked wearing a lover's cast-off clothes: softened with wear and not exactly laundry fresh. Being surrounded by a familiar male scent felt curiously intimate.

He led her down to his office on the ground floor overlooking the lush, well-kept lawns sweeping down to the lazy river. She'd only been in here once or twice before, and always under the hawk-like eye of his PA. A Sunday morning was different.

Peter turned on the computer. Lia came and sat

on his lap, reaching through the gaping neckline of his dressing gown to toy with his chest hair again. She was leaning against his right arm and perhaps he had to type more slowly than he would normally. She was running her tongue up and down the side of his neck – a little salty and musky from a night's sleep and the eager reunion sex that had preceded it. But all the while she was looking at the keyboard out of the corner of her eye. So that was his password. Hmm. Not difficult to memorise.

He called up some sites. They scrolled through pictures of heavy-breasted women wearing tight, black, wet-look style bustiers that were obviously just that little bit too small for them. Lia felt her own arousal stirring again. Was it the thought of wearing something like that herself? Or was she feeling turned on by the women in the photographs?

She shifted her weight slightly on Peter's lap. Just enough to discover that his erection was pumping up again.

'I thought you were after something lacy and romantic,' he murmured as she took control of the mouse and began opening pictures of women in red and black PVC corsets that bound in their waists and thrust up their breasts into exaggerated domes.

'It's a girlie's prerogative to change her mind. And anyway, I've seen what effect these have on you. Or rather, I've felt it.'

She shifted her weight a little again, rubbing her bare buttocks – the T-shirt had rode up – against his silk-covered lap. He was as hard as a metal rod now. But it was a delicious sensation, that hardness and the cool, slithery fabric that was keeping it from touching her tender naked skin.

'Just remember I have the last word,' he grunted against her shoulder. 'He who pays the piper calls the tune and all that.'

'Whatever. I'm very broad-minded. I promise to wear it.'

'Then give me that bloody mouse back.'

She was genuinely surprised at what he chose. An ivory-silk teddy with antique lace trim. It was exquisite. It was tasteful. But after the black leather dominatrix gear they'd seen, Lia couldn't help feeling it was a bit of a let down.

'I'm surprised,' she said, as he keyed in his credit card details; she didn't look – she wasn't interested in that. 'I thought you'd take a walk on the wilder side.'

'Patience. I'll bring you something like that back from Amsterdam. But I rather fancy you wearing that teddy under your waitress's uniform when you're at work here. I'd like to imagine you walking around with it on under your clothes. Anything darker or kinkier would show under than tight little white blouse. Now,' the computer made the jerky, electronic machine-gun-type noise as he logged off, 'can we go back to bed?'

Lia turned to face him on the swivel chair. She eased aside his dark dressing gown and peeled her borrowed T-shirt up and over her head. Her breasts bounced free just level with his face. Sitting face-to-face like this, she thought, I bet I could take his thick cock really, really deep.

They never did make it back to the bedroom.

With the efficiency of on-line shopping, the pack-

134

age arrived for her on the following Tuesday morning. Lia tried it on at once. It fitted perfectly over her bust but seemed just a fraction long in the body. The delicate button fastening dangled an inch or so below her bush. It gave her the strange sensation that she wasn't wearing anything down there at all.

She walked backwards and forwards a few times in her room to try it out. On reflection, she rather liked the feeling. Especially on a warm day like today. The conference delegates would be out on the lawns during their break times and she could walk among them with her trays of drinks and salty canapés, a slight breeze creeping up her short black skirt and tickling her quim.

Lia pulled on the rest of her uniform quickly. Who were they catering for today, anyway? She had to admit, she'd kept track of Peter's where-abouts more assiduously than she'd memorised their conference guests. So she had to think for a moment. Ah yes, some one-day seminar on promoting rural tourism.

Any novelty the job might have held had worn off by now. She knew how to smile non-threateningly at the seminar guests, take their drinks orders and move on. They weren't as real to her as the everyday punters she'd flirted with through the hatch of the *Lady Jayne*. So she was on autopilot that afternoon, threading her way through the men – and very occasional woman – in sombre business suits on the lawn. She was thinking more about the delicious little wafts of air that were sneaking in through the opening of her teddy. And she was wondering if it would feel even naughtier if, the next time she was out of sight, she undid those three little pearly buttons altogether.

She wasn't expecting someone to catch her arm on her way back to the kitchen and she nearly spilt a tray of half-empty wine glasses when he did.

'Lia, you've got your head in the clouds today. Didn't you see me?'

For a moment she couldn't take it in. His curly, tousled hair was a bit longer now. Hadn't he been taking care of himself? His clothes were smart, but casual – no match for the other delegates' executive suits. Trust Denny. He never had known what to wear in order to fit in. All he knew how to do was, well, what he did.

'What on earth are you doing here?' she whispered.

'Rural tourism – that's me, isn't it?' Then he grinned sheepishly and looked down at his shoes. She noticed they were scuffed. 'Yeah, well, it's not exactly what I was expecting. All high flown, clever stuff. Not about me running my pub. Old Holme-Lacey dropped by the other night and was touting for business so I thought, It's a quiet day, Mike can hold the fort again and I might as well give it a go. At least I got to see you though.' He winked.

'Peter was in the Boatman's Rest?' That had never occurred to her. But then, he never revealed what he did with his time when he wasn't at his rambling Georgian home.

'Yeah, he's been popping in quite regularly. Keeps asking where I'm hiding my beautiful wife.' He nudged her. 'You wouldn't believe the number of pottery evening-classes and visits to your sister in London you've had these last few weeks. Sorry, I know you don't look like a pottery evening-class person. It was the best I could think of on the spot.'

It took Lia a moment or two to sort out the tangle of feelings. Part of her was bubbling. She'd really pulled the deception off. But she was furious, too. Peter was going off sniffing around another woman. But that woman, Miranda, was *her*. She'd never been jealous of herself before . . .

'So it's true he's got you working here while the boat's fixed? What's it like? The punters don't half miss you.'

'And what about the landlord?'

'He can't cook as well and he doesn't look anything like as good in a crop top and cut-off jeans. Seriously, Li. When are the three of you back on the move again?'

'Good question. Trudi's going so stir crazy here I don't trust her with the chopping knife. Jules has moved in with Jonathan; thinks we're a couple of spineless sell-outs and has got a job in some trendy veggie café it's going to be hell to prise her out of.'

'And you?'

'I'm coping.'

'But you can't wait to be back on the *Lady Jayne* again?'

Until he'd said it, she wouldn't have been able to predict her answer. For all Trudi's reservations, Lia had felt safe here. Protected from the big outside world for the first time in her life. Safe from having to make any difficult decisions. It had been like a holiday. But looking into Denny's hazel eyes, remembering how his unkempt hair felt under her fingertips, knowing how mischievous his smile was first thing in the morning and how warm the curve of his shoulder felt . . . Everything she loved about her real, roving life came flooding back.

'I can't wait to get out of here.'

'Any chance you're finished for the day?' He glanced at his watch and then over his shoulder. The other seminar guests were drifting back towards their conference rooms. 'I really think I can give the last workshop on EU legislation a miss.'

'There's no more food to serve but Trudi and I need to clear up.'

'Can she spare you for an hour or so? We could take a walk along the river. It's been so long since I've seen you, Li.' He touched her arm. If she hadn't been holding on to the tray she would have hugged him. Her eyes were open again. And she'd missed him more than she'd ever realised.

'I've just got to lose this. Give me five minutes.'

Lia hurried back to the kitchens. Trudi was already busy loading the dishwasher. When Lia grabbed a left-over bottle of Chardonnay, Trudi raised one eyebrow in surprise, but Lia didn't have time to say anything before the kitchen door opened and there was Peter's sharp-faced PA ushering in a man they both recognised.

'Paul Gillespie, Environmental Health Department, South Warwickshire—' He was about to flash his laminated photocard at them, then stopped. 'Ah. I wasn't expecting to see you two.'

'You're more used to dealing with this sort of thing, aren't you, Trudi?' Lia said sweetly, snatching a couple of clean glasses to go with the Chardonnay. 'I'll catch you later.'

Without pausing to care what either Trudi, Gillespie, or the waspish PA thought, Lia slipped past them and out of the back door. She brandished the wine and glasses at Denny.

'Let's get out of sight fast,' she said. 'Anywhere you had in mind?'

'I was hoping you'd tell me. You must have been here over a month now. You've probably walked every footpath in a ten mile radius, if I know you.'

But she hadn't. She hadn't even been off Peter Holme-Lacey's territory. Had she really become so insular?

'Let's just follow the river and see what happens. Then we can find somewhere quiet to finish this. It's good stuff.'

'I know. I also know the wine merchant who stitches him up on the price for it.'

They both chuckled. There was something about the thought of someone else getting one over on the seemingly all-powerful Peter Holme-Lacey. They clambered over the fence that marked the boundary and after that Denny took her free hand. It was easy to forget Peter had ever been her lover. That had belonged to another time. This, here, walking in the sun with a man whose warm, solid body she knew so well: this was real life.

There was a cooler breeze. There always was by the river. It snaked under her skirt and caressed her labia where the silky teddy didn't quite meet her flesh. A free-in-the-breeze kind of sensuality took over. She really wished she'd had time to undo the buttons and let the fresh air stroke her pussy to the utmost.

After about another half a mile they came to a clump of crack willows shading a sandy bank by a curve in the river. One great bough of a willow had fallen long before. They sat down on it and Denny poured the Chardonnay. As he did so he cupped his other hand over hers, holding her glass to keep it steady. She felt herself tremble this close to him.

'Remind me,' he said, 'did I always have this effect on you?'

'It's been a long time.'

'We've been apart for a month or more before.'

'A lot's happened. And I've been stupid. Jules is right. I took an easy option and I'm not proud about that. Things are looking clearer now.' She reached up and kissed him. 'And I have missed you.'

He chuckled into her hair. 'I won't ask. About this "lots" that's "happened", I mean. I don't need to know everything.'

'I know. That's what's great about you.' She rested her head against his chest. She could hear his heart beating – a little faster than a gentle walk would account for. She began playing with the front of his casual, brushed-cotton shirt. It had a welcoming feel to it. 'And I'm glad you didn't turn up in a suit like all the other men. You're you and you're supposed to look like you. I'm rapidly going off men in suits.'

'The way I remember it, you don't approve of your men wearing suits – or anything else come to that.'

Her hands crept in between the buttons of his shirt and caressed the curve of his pec muscles. Yes, there was something about the excitement of new lovers: the chemistry, the thrill, the undiscovered territory. But there was something to be said for the warmth and familiarity of old lovers, too. An intimate knowledge of each other's bodies, each other's responses.

She ran her other hand up over his broad back. His stretched shirt was so invitingly soft. Between his shoulder blades was one of those little tags that are often on casual shirts for no apparent reason. 'So you can hang me up when you're finished with me,' Denny had once joked in a close, tender moment. As if. Time together had given them a history of erotic memories to draw on. Like right now she could visualise Denny's chest beneath his soft shirt. She knew its texture, even its taste if she chose to run the tip of her tongue over his nipples and down his flanks. And that would provoke a predictable response. But predictable wasn't always bad.

'I hope you didn't suggest this walk just as an excuse to seduce me in the open air,' she said, sliding her hand more fully between his buttons and flipping a few of them open.

'Oh? Don't tell me you've gone all shy and only-in-the-bedroom on me.'

'No.' With her other hand she picked up her wine glass again and downed what was left of the Chardonnay. It had warmed up during the walk but it was still crisp, fresh and just light enough to be perfect for drinking in the afternoon. 'But if anyone's going to be doing the seducing, it's me, okay?'

'Thank goodness for that.' He grinned that grin she couldn't resist. It was full and warm and she hadn't realised how much she'd been subconsciously looking for it in Peter's cooler, enigmatic smiles. 'I promise not to resist. Well, not too loudly.'

She drew her lips over his prominent Adam's apple and kissed her way round to whisper in his ear. 'Did you know that underneath this I'm only wearing a rather naughty silk teddy?'

'I thought you weren't wearing a bra. Things were on the move a bit while we were walking along.'

'It unbuttons at the crotch. You could undo it and fuck me without taking off any of my clothes. In fact, it's a bit loose down there. You could even slip the material aside and fuck me without undoing anything.'

That kind of thought usually gave Denny an instant hard-on. She slid her hand back out of his shirt and moved it down to the front of his trousers. He was wearing some dark cords that weren't particularly trendy. But they were deliciously tight on his arse. And they moulded themselves around an erection that was particularly hard to ignore.

'You must be kidding,' he whispered. 'I've been living like a monk for so long I want to *see* you. All of you. Especially if you're wearing something naughty. As if this little waitress's uniform wasn't enough of a fantasy.'

He began unbuttoning her close-fitting blouse. When he'd peeled it down off her shoulders he gave a low, appreciative chuckle at the flimsiness of the ivory-silk teddy beneath. Not even Peter had seen her wearing it yet. A shiver of rebelliousness went through her at that thought. His might have had the gold credit card that paid for it but another man was enjoying it first.

And then there wasn't time to even think about that. Denny lowered his head and began kissing along the lacy neckline. The beginnings of stubble on his chin felt abrasive as he stroked it against the upper curves of her breasts. But excitingly so. Denny's stubble always came back within hours of a shave. Must have a lot of testosterone pumping around.

The fabric was so fine. She could feel his lips seeking her flesh but at the same time he was removed from her. Contact but not contact. He moved lower and began kissing her nipples through the wispy silk, even using his tongue round and round her tightening, peaking buds. The fabric was dampening as he licked and sucked, moulding itself even closer to her hardening breasts. But though she could feel his lips and tongue working on her, working her into a frenzy, she couldn't feel their real texture. It was the kind of stimulation you might get from a particularly erotic dream: enough to arouse you but infuriating because it didn't take you all the way.

'I must be wet,' she sighed, 'because you are driving me so crazy.'

He slipped one hand up her short black skirt, eased aside the silky teddy and fingered her warm quim. 'You are. Juicy as anything. Let's go for it.'

She shifted her weight and let him unzip the tight skirt. Then he tugged the all-in-one creamy silk up and over her head. Her breasts bounced slightly as they came free of the delicate lingerie. She stood up before him. He ran his hands over her firm figure.

'God, I've missed you,' he whispered. 'You're so warm. So solid. All woman.'

'Then what are you waiting for? Show me how much you've missed me.'

Most of his shirt buttons were already undone. Denny yanked the others apart and tossed the shirt aside. He stood up in order to ease his zip down over his bulging crotch. He always seemed to wear trousers with chunky brass zips, not fiddly, flimsy things. She'd often thought it was because he needed something solid to keep that much manhood in check.

Lia knelt before him and helped him slide down his underwear. Solid hipster briefs – nothing fancy. Basic masculinity was what you got with Denny.

As she slipped them down his erection sprang out and bounced against her cheek. She kissed it and ran her nose and lips along its stout length, taking in the tangy, male scent she loved so well. She moved to engulf his cock head in her willing mouth but Denny laid a hand on her coppery hair.

'I'm too close,' he murmured. 'You're turning me on too much – just looking at you after all this time. I want to bury myself deep in that warm, special part of you. I want to hold back enough to give you a fantastic time.'

There was a pile of their discarded clothes already draped over the fallen willow bough. He sat back on these. She sat astride him, welcoming his ramrod cock so deep into her it seemed to fill the whole centre of her body. All her awareness centred round his hot maleness.

This was how she'd made love to Peter the last time. But the thought was no more than fleeting. With Denny it was so different even though, superficially, the mechanics might be the same. The feeling wasn't. Lia wasn't playing games now. Whatever the excitement with Peter, however much the power play between them might give her feelings an edge, there was a tenderness here he could never match.

She began to move her hips. The movement was subtle. She felt his stiff cock glide up and down within her moist tunnel. The gentle pressure of her greedy clit against his body each time she sank fully down on to his lap. Gentler than a tongue or finger's stimulation. Enough to make for a long slow ride towards orgasm.

Denny cupped her breasts in his hands. They'd hardened with desire under his kisses and tongue flicks. Her nipples were peaking buds between his fingertips. She was proud of their firmness. She arched her back as she rode him, thrusting her breasts further towards his face. He grinned as he fondled them, clearly aroused by the sight.

His cock inside her was like a pivot for her whole being. His erection was so incredibly sure. She could well believe he'd been saving himself for weeks for this.

She did a slow dance around his iron hardness. She rolled her hips in a figure of eight pattern – delicious stimulation for her but an infuriating tease for him. She did it just long enough to feel the tension mount inside her, nudging her that little bit further towards her climax and then she changed her rhythm again, riding him up and down, the fast and furious way she knew he liked his cock to be pleasured. As his mouth fell open and little involuntary gasps escaped him she slowed right down again, taking him to the brink and then switching back to her own pleasure.

Lia must have done this four or five times. Denny's eyes were screwed tight shut now, the look of frustration yet delight clear on his face. This time Lia softly closed her eyes. She ground herself against him as close as two bodies could be. The first tiny ripples of the long-denied orgasm began chasing each other around the tops of her thighs, over her plump mons and then deep, deep into the core of her sex. While she was still possessed by those delicious waves she began riding Denny like crazy. The piston action prolonged her own sweet climax. He cried out loud and she felt him come inside her. She clamped her well-trained muscles tight against him, savouring every nuance of his explosion within her.

Afterwards, breathless, they laid their heads on each other's shoulders. It had grown a little cooler now. The persistent breeze from the river hadn't troubled her before but now its tendrils coiled round her damp, bare body. She shivered.

'We'd better get back. Trudi will be after my blood.'

Reluctantly she got off his lap and began to collect her things. As she retrieved the empty Chardonnay bottle and glasses she said, 'Better do our bit for the environment and take these back for recycling – keep Jules happy.' Then she noticed the ivory silk teddy. It had fallen to the ground too near the river and there was a mud stain across one flank. 'Ah. That could take a bit of explaining.'

She met Denny's eyes. He didn't say anything but she could read his look of sadness. He wasn't innocent. He'd long known about Jonathan. Now he knew there was someone else – someone who bought her delicate lingerie – but there was nothing he could do to hold her back.

They walked back hand in hand to Peter's mansion. When they got to the kitchens none of the clearing up had been done and Trudi was nowhere to be seen.

'I'd better make myself scarce,' Denny sighed.

'All the suits have gone home by now. I don't want to get you into trouble or anything.'

'I'll show you the quickest way out.'

But as she was coming back from showing Denny a side entrance she heard voices coming from the PA's office. One of them was Trudi's distinctive South African twang. Lia hovered by the half-open door.

'We've never had a warning notice like this before,' the PA was protesting.

'That's as may be, but you've got one now,' replied a familiar male voice. Lia couldn't see its owner. 'Your meat freezer temperatures rose above an acceptable level. I expect you to locate and rectify the fault before my next visit. I'll see you then.'

'Wait. You'll need to speak to Mr Holme-Lacey about this. He's due back from Oxford any time now.'

'I'm sure you're capable of passing on the message. Isn't that what he pays you for? Goodbye.'

The man swept out past Lia. She realised it was the environmental health inspector – but in a more assertive mode than he'd ever shown aboard the *Lady Jayne*. Trudi followed close behind him, smirking that smirk Lia had come to recognise.

'Okay, what happened?' she demanded when they'd shut the kitchen door behind them. 'And I don't just mean the hygiene regulations – although I thought we were on top of that.'

'We are, Li. But if you leave a meat freezer open for long in order to shag someone's brains out up against it, the temperature's bound to rise.'

'*What?*'

'You heard.' Trudi chuckled as she ran a wine glass against her neck. She seemed to be enjoying the cool, hard texture. 'And to think I've spent the best part of a year trying to work out what lit that guy's candle. He's got a fetish about cold things, obviously.' With her free hand she rubbed her back. 'And I've probably got ice burns all up and down but, hey, it was worth it. It was wild.' She winked. 'And an official warning will rattle old Holme-Lacey's cage.'

'And show us up in a bad light.'

Trudi was about to say something when the kitchen door opened. Peter stood there with the Inspector's notice in his hand.

'This is your responsibility. I hope for your sakes you run things better on my barge than you do in my house.'

Trudi drew herself up to her full height. She could look him straight in the eye that way. 'Actually, it's not. We're self-employed contractors; the premises and equipment are your responsibility. And if your equipment's not up to the job we can't help that.'

She's her old self again, Lia thought. She's coming out fighting. And she's been so bored cooped up here she's been hitting Peter's state-of-the-art multi-gym hard. Those curves look more fantastic than they ever did.

Peter didn't speak for a moment. His face was darkening but Trudi took advantage and pressed on. 'And speaking of our barge, isn't it about time she was ready?'

Peter's jaw moved backwards and forwards as if chewing over his words before he spat them out. 'That's the other thing I was coming to tell you. I called in at the boatyard on my way back. The *Lady Jayne* is operational again. Someone will bring her upriver tomorrow morning and you can start off again from here.' He put down the Inspector's notice, reached into an inner jacket pocket and took out another folded paper. 'This is your new itinerary. I've booked you in to cater for some contacts of mine. You'll need these higher paying venues to meet the lease payments on the barge. Especially as I'll have to revise those payments upwards to cover the recent repairs.'

Trudi snatched the paper from him. Lia read over her shoulder. Her stomach tightened as she did. Business conventions. More men in dark suits. And the regional AGM of a political party that would have Jules throwing a fit.

'All those details will, incidentally, be up on your new website,' Peter continued. 'I've had space created for you under my corporate web pages. It's important for a group of companies to put forward a unified and professional image. Those irrelevant adverts on your pages – property development firms and such like – just create a patchwork impression. So I suggest you phone that web monkey of yours and have the old site closed down. After all, security wasn't very good on it, was it?' He looked at them coldly. 'I prefer to believe it was a hacking problem that kept me from catching up with you in the first place. Saves everyone embarrassment.'

Lia met his eyes. He was all ruthlessness now. There was no recognition of her as a person, as his lover. The realisation hit her: business and winning were everything to Peter Holme-Lacey. She couldn't believe she'd ever taken to his bed.

'I expect you've got a lot of packing to do, being girls.' Then he gestured at the state of the kitchen. 'Not to mention clearing up here – as if one warning wasn't enough. I'll leave you to get on with it.'

Lia sighed heavily and flopped down on a chair after he'd gone. 'How did that happen? I thought we had the upper hand for a moment and then he turns it back on us.' She gestured at the list of dates and places Trudi was still reading. 'And how come you're so calm about it?'

'Let him crow a little now. It doesn't matter. Because we're going to stitch him up.' She sat down across the table from Lia and looked her straight in the eye. 'We *are* going to stitch him up, aren't we, Li?'

CHAPTER

9

_____

By mid-morning Trudi was happily clanging doors in the narrow galley, making sure everything was as it should be. She opened one cupboard right above the stove. An avalanche of small cardboard boxes fell into her arms.

'If you would only stick to one type of tea,' Lia commented, helping her retrieve the various packets, 'we could save a lot of space in here!'

'Spoilsport. You know I like variety. Some mornings I need a big strong Assam to slap me around a bit and wake me up, then again in the afternoons I like a subtle, ever-so-slightly spiced Rooibos. I have to keep my options open.'

Lia crammed the last box of a herbal blend into a space beside the organic Darjeeling. 'Are we still talking about tea now?'

Trudi grinned. 'Go figure.'

Lia realised she hadn't seen Trudi grin quite that wide for a long time. Certainly not since they'd found themselves holed up *chez* Peter Holme-Lacey. But things were different this morning.

151

Even the air had a fresher feel to it. They were about to be on the move again. And, Lia realised, Trudi really did have a devastating smile.

'Sorry about the way I was back there,' she began. 'I was pretty spineless for a while. Jules had a point. But it's tempting – the idea of someone else, some father figure taking the responsibility for everything. I let myself get seduced.'

'Don't beat yourself up over it. We're back in business now. And if he thinks we're going to play his game . . .' Trudi gave her a slap on the shoulder. But it was nothing more than matey. Lia wasn't sure whether to be disappointed or not. 'Come on. We've wasted enough time hanging round here. Get your backside up on deck and we'll cast off. If we push it we can be at Jonathan's this evening and pick up the third weird sister.'

They made good time to Jonathan's. When they let themselves in, he was lounging in front of his computer wearing a short, red kimono-type dressing gown and little else. Lia's pulse quickened. She thought of all the games she'd like to play, reacquainting herself with that lithe, oh-so-holdable body when business was out of the way.

'Your security's crap,' Trudi stated, 'if we could just walk in here. What would all those clients whose web sites you host think of that? Anyway, where's Jules?'

'At work, of course. Not that she's here much when she isn't at the café bar. Practically lives with Lynne downstairs. You know – the new tenant. The one *you* rather liked . . . ?'

Lia watched Trudi. A muscle flickered in her temple but otherwise she was giving nothing away. What was needling her? The fact that Jules had muscled in on someone she'd fancied herself? But they'd shared lovers in the past; they seemed to enjoy the kinkiness of it. The fact that Jules had a cosy live-in relationship with someone else? Or was she just peeved because Jonathan had bitten straight back after her 'security' dig?

'I'll take you round to the famous "Vegetable Love", shall I?' Jonathan continued. We could all grab a bite to eat there.' He began shutting down the computer. 'I wasn't doing anything important – just some new banner ads for my uncle.' He reached up and squeezed Lia's arm. 'It'll be good. I've missed you.'

He dived through into the bedroom and changed. When he came out again a moment later he'd tied back his purple-streaked hair and was wearing a T-shirt, sandals and the sort of loose, baggy batik shorts that only really lean men with perfect buttocks can get away with. Following him closely down the long stairs, Lia reached a hand down and fondled his butt as he walked. It was hard and beautiful in her hand. She loved the way it tensed and relaxed as he moved. Knowing Jonathan, she wondered what he was wearing under those shorts. Something of hers, even? The thought intrigued her.

The café bar was in an old part of town, down a flight of stone stairs, with moody lighting, all retro chic with intricate leaf patterns stencilled on the walls. They nabbed a table for four and ordered spicy-bean tortilla wraps while they waited for Jules to take a break.

A woman walked by – a small, trim woman with neat-bobbed red hair. She had a confidence and familiarity with the bar as if she was more than a regular customer, but not staff. Jonathan leaned across the table and whispered in Lia's ear, 'That's Lynne.'

As Lynne came level with their table she turned and seemed to recognise Trudi. 'Hey,' she said, leaning on the back of Trudi's chair, 'I've got a bone to pick with you.'

Trudi had to twist round to talk to her. It put her on the back foot. Lia wasn't used to seeing her friend like that.

'I know,' she said and patted Lynne's hand. 'They're all safe aboard the *Lady Jayne*. We just, er, took a little detour getting back to you.'

'So I heard.'

'If you're going to the kitchens, will you tell Jules to hurry up?'

Now what was all that about? Lia wondered. But she didn't wonder for long. Under the table, Jonathan's leg was brushing her own. It was so good to feel his skin against hers. It had been so long. She stretched her own legs further into the dark, secret space between his. She hitched up her cotton skirt a little. Her smooth legs snaked against his hairier ones. The contrast was delicious.

Their tortilla wraps came. Trudi bit into hers enthusiastically and said with a full mouth, 'Hey, this is good. I taught Jules to make this dressing,' but Lia and Jonathan weren't really listening.

He'd slipped off his sandals. He was running his big toe around her inner ankle bone. With the mules she was wearing he could just about make the full circuit, teasing his toe pad into the hollow below her ankle bone. Lia stopped chewing her second bite of tortilla. Even though the hot, tangy sauce was firing on her taste buds her attention was down below. Ankles were an unexpectedly sexy place.

Or maybe it wasn't that unexpected. She remembered at college being chatted up by a guy who did reflexology sessions on the side. He'd told her the areas on the insides and outsides of each ankle corresponded to the sex organs. And then he'd proceeded to give her a thoroughly convincing demonstration. One thing was for sure, Jonathan's probing toe was sending shivers of pleasure up the inside of each leg. He teased one ankle bone and then the other. And the place where the resultant shivers met was becoming very moist and horny.

Lia kicked off her shoes under the table. She began running the tops of her feet up along the backs of his muscular calves. His hairiness tickled her. Then she wriggled her bare feet further up still. And she realised why it was so wonderful that Jonathan was wearing baggy shorts tonight. His thighs were spread wide under the table. She could just about sneak a small foot up inside his shorts and touch his tense crotch.

All the time they kept eye contact. Above the table, everything was still. They hardly even touched their food. Trudi was demolishing hers with typical gusto and muttering all the time about the quality and freshness of the salad garnish, but they paid her no more attention than if she'd been a stranger chattering at the next table.

Lia snaked her big toe along his bulging pouch. The texture she felt was a silky-slippery one but unfamiliar. The material was too thick for it to be some of her own borrowed lingerie. What could it be?

Beneath the fabric she chased the yielding outline of his balls. But she couldn't quite feel the length of his cock. Her leg was aching from holding it at this unfamiliar angle. Her hamstring muscles were burning from being overstretched. But the novelty of feeling Jonathan up in public like this took priority over everything.

His cock was already erect – she was sure of that. But it was leaning over towards his opposite hip, trapped in its silky-mystery prison. She couldn't foot-fondle it from this angle. She drew her foot out, sliding it down his hairy inner thighs and glided it back into the other side of his shorts. They both gasped as she made contact with his bulging erection under its tight, slippery fabric.

'All right, guys.' Jules yanked out the fourth empty chair, turned it round and sat astride it, cowboy fashion. 'I can give you ten minutes. What's so urgent you had to send a waitress in and then two minutes later Lynne to chase me up?'

Lia sighed and pulled her foot away from Jonathan's groin. She knew, practically, she couldn't have brought him off like that. But the abrupt interruption to their tantalising game left her shaking.

Fortunately Trudi seemed to have taken over. 'The *Lady Jayne*'s as good as new. No, better, even. And she's moored up not ten minutes' walk from here.'

'Hope you locked her up well, then, if she's in this part of town.'

'Be serious. Are you coming back with us?'

'Trudi, I can't just walk out on this job and leave them in the lurch. Besides . . .' She glanced round the bar as if she was looking for someone.

'You walked out on us. Well, all right – but you didn't exactly let us know you were going to take this one.'

Jules leaned forwards and banged her head softly against the chair-back. 'You're going to guilt-trip me into this, aren't you? Remind me of all the time we've been together, the all-for-one-and-one-for-all stuff?'

'Hey, you just saved me the effort.' Trudi grinned. That grin took no prisoners. Lia could almost see Jules melting under it. 'Jules, we need you. It's going to be good again – just like it was. But you're an important part of that.'

'We've got bookings?'

'High-paying ones. Look.' Trudi handed her the schedule.

'Rotarians. Some up-market wedding. And the – oh no, I'm not cooking for *them*.'

'We'll be out from under Holme-Lacey's thumb by then. But we need you to do it.'

'I said I'd help you stitch him up. I didn't say . . . Oh hell. I'll sleep on it, okay? Now I really have to get back to the kitchens. And I'll be late home. You can head back with Lynne but don't wait up for me.'

They took her advice. The streets were fully dark by then but the night was still warm. Trudi and Lynne walked on in front. They seemed edgy with each other and it wasn't surprising: Lynne had got cosy with Jules and now Trudi had come to take her away. With the edginess was a spark, though. Jonathan leaned close to Lia and commented on it.

'They're not going to miss us if we drop behind,' he finished.

'What did you have in mind?'

'You were feeling me up. We got interrupted.'

'You've got a nice comfortable futon back home.'

'Where's your sense of adventure?'

'Weirdo.'

'I know. And you love me for it.'

Trudi and Lynne were half a street ahead of them now and didn't even seem to have noticed. Jonathan pulled her into an unlit side alley.

'What are you wearing underneath those shorts?' she whispered. 'It's been bugging me all evening.'

'Something you won't have seen yet. I ordered it on the web just the other day. No, it's meant for blokes, honestly. A wet-look thong, all silky and shimmery and this lovely turquoise green.'

'Mmm, a thong.' She turned to face him and cupped both his firm buttocks in her hands. 'That explains why I can't feel anything on your gorgeous arse.'

She squeezed for a few more moments. Just touching Jonathan's body was enough to get her going again. She replayed the sexy feelings she'd experienced in the bar when he'd run his bare toe round and round her ankle bone. The warmth rose in her quim again at the thought of such a public grope.

'Pretend I'm a whore,' she stretched up and whispered in his ear. She knew Jonathan sometimes fantasised about doing it with a prostitute – something he never could do in real life. He needed tenderness and trust for sex and you couldn't buy that.

'Did I pick you up, or did you pick me up?'

'I picked you up. You were in a bar you never

normally go to. Some of your mates were supposed to meet you there but they didn't show up. You were feeling vulnerable. Alone. Then I saw you looking at me. You knew just what I was and you were itching to get inside my pants. I knew you wouldn't make the first move, though. You were too inexperienced. Too nervous. Didn't know the right things to say. So I came over and took the matter into my own hands.'

'How are we going to do it?'

'Oh, you really are an innocent, aren't you? We're going to do it up against this wall. Here. Standing up. A quickie. That's how you fuck a whore. And no, don't kiss me. Don't even undress me more than you have to. Just make my legs tremble as you thrust it in.'

As Lia said this her hands moved round to the front of his shorts. She slipped the elasticated waistband down. Her fingers moulded over the slithery pouch of his thong. It was well filled with his erection and tensed up balls. For a while she just let her hands glide over the enticing fabric, glancing down once or twice to see that, yes, it really was a metallic turquoise and the streetlight opposite their alley gleamed on it. Jonathan moaned at her touch. She could feel his cock straining and dampening, making that little give-away spot high on the pouch. She slipped his thong down and his warm cock tumbled out into her willing hands.

She held back from fondling him – much as she loved the feel of his bare prick in her hands. This might be a quickie up against the wall but she didn't want him coming too soon. She was looking forward to the ride.

Jonathan was rucking up her cotton skirt and fumbling with her panties. Soon he'd reached her pussy, which was moist and had been moistening all evening ready for him. It was good that Jonathan wasn't much taller than her. Their hips were virtually level. He slid into her and it was so sweet and easy to fuck standing up.

When he was in deep, he began wrestling her T-shirt up until it was above her breasts. He didn't bother unclipping her bra, though. She was wearing one that was seamfree, translucent and fitted like a second skin. Just right to wear beneath a skimpy T-shirt on a hot summer night: no seam lines and the fabric was so thin it let her excited nipples show. As Jonathan fondled her breasts through the fine material, she might as well have been wearing no bra at all.

'This sort of fucking could get you arrested,' she whispered in his ear as he drove into her. He'd taken her at her word – a quickie. There was no finesse to his rhythm – he was racing to come. But she was excited by the novelty, the danger, too. The whole length of her vagina was buzzing with it. Her own orgasm wasn't far off. 'Or maybe you'd like to be arrested?' she continued. 'Does the thought of being roughed up and taken away by a big, burly policeman turn you on?'

Jonathan's thrusts became almost violent. She knew she'd touched a nerve. As with so many things, she knew Jonathan would never go with another man – but he loved the decadence of fantasising about it. And he'd shared all those fantasies with her.

'Would you like him to pin your arms behind your back and handcuff you?' she continued, realising that the fantasy was turning her on more and more. 'Would you like him to strip search you, even though there's no need? How about making it a little more intimate? Would you like him to bend you over and slip his rubber gloved finger deep into your arse? Or perhaps you'd rather it was something hornier than his finger?'

Lia bit her lip at how far she'd allowed her imagination to go. The thought of Jonathan submitting to another man was rioting in her head. She hadn't realised it could excite her so much. As tender as she felt towards Jonathan – even love in a funny, freewheeling kind of way – the thought of a dominant, macho man doing to him what Peter Holme-Lacey had done to her over his carved, wooden bedstead aroused her out of all proportion. Behind her closed eyes she played out the scene: Jonathan's tight, virgin arsehole taking in a big man's bullish cock while she stood and watched and slipped her own fingers down inside her pants. The fantasy brought her to a sudden, jolting orgasm.

Jonathan groaned – she wondered if he felt cheated at her managing to come so quickly – and speeded up his thrusts. She simply enjoyed their fury now. Her body was like a rag doll's between his ramming body and the hard wall. But she loved the feel of his cock inside her, moving faster as it drove towards its climax. Then he cried out loud and spasmed inside her.

They both took a moment to catch their breath. Coming back to reality now, Lia tensed every time she heard a sound. Jonathan had cried out so loud when he'd climaxed she was scared they'd attracted someone's attention. But no one came looking for them. Jonathan held her tight, his cock still firmly inside her and, finally, he kissed her.

'That'll be something to remember,' he whispered. 'You're amazing.'

'I know. But we'd better get back to your flat. Trudi will be wondering where we are.'

'Oh, she'll have invited herself into Lynne's for 'coffee'. You can count on it.'

But when they got back to the tall, Gothic Victorian building and climbed to the top floor, Trudi was slumped, miffed, outside Jonathan's front door.

'What kept you guys?' she demanded. 'On second thoughts, don't tell me. And wipe those grins off your faces. Is everyone getting laid tonight except me?'

At ten o'clock the next morning Trudi checked her watch for the seventh time and sighed. 'Okay. We've fed those ever-present swans more stale bread than is good for them and given Jules half an hour more than we said. She's not coming. Let's cast off.'

Lia went up on deck, began undoing the ropes and shooshed away the two swans who thought they'd won the bread roll lottery. But there was no enthusiasm. This should have been a new beginning – the three of them back together again. It had fallen flat. How were they going to make it work without Jules?

'Maybe we do need Holme-Lacey after all,' she said later as Trudi brought her a coffee and they switched over on the tiller, 'if there's only going to be the two of us. It would be a lot easier to keep our heads down and tow the line.'

'We've been through this. If we're at some rich bastard's beck and call then what's the point of doing it at all? We started this whole thing up to be independent.'

'Yeah, but we had Jules then. She's not only one third of the cooking team, she understands the accounts and stuff. I don't think we can do it without her.'

'We can learn that stuff ourselves.'

'Yeah. When?'

They went quiet and sipped their cooling coffees for a while. Eventually Trudi said, 'Li, is there any law about riding motorbikes on the towpath?'

'Dunno. Why?'

'Look back there. Some bloody idiot's bombing along behind us. They're yelling at us, too.'

'Idiots,' Lia agreed without enthusiasm.

The motorbike drew level with them, overshot by twenty yards or so then screeched to a halt. The small pillion passenger leaped off and yanked aside her helmet.

'Don't you two ever listen when someone's telling you to stop?'

'Jules!'

Trudi crunched the throttle into reverse. Lia grabbed the ropes and leaped on to the towpath, lashing the first to a convenient tree root as she didn't have time to bang in a stake.

'So,' Lia said when they'd all come to a complete stop, 'someone going to tell me what's happening?'

'I overslept.' Jules rubbed the side of her little uptilted nose, the way she did when she was lying. Lia let it pass. 'When I got down to the bridge where you said you'd moored, you'd already left.

163

So I dashed back to the flat to get Lynne to give me a ride. Took a while to figure out which way you'd gone.'

By now Lynne had taken off her own helmet and was shaking out her auburn bob, which wasn't quite so neat this morning. The young woman looked as if she was trying to stay out of things. It must, Lia thought, have been a difficult decision for her to give Jules that lift.

'Well, you're here now. Let's get moving,' Trudi said. 'Hop aboard and – oh, hang on a sec.' She dived below deck and came out a few seconds later with a holdall, which she passed across to Lynne waiting on the bank. 'Thanks for the loan. I've taken good care of them.'

Jules and Lynne had a long hug goodbye. Trudi pointedly wasn't looking. Then Jules jumped on board and Lynne's bike roared off.

'I'm surprised at her riding her motorbike along the towpath,' Lia commented, 'being a traffic warden and all. What's so funny?'

'Nothing. Now I'm here, what can I do?' Jules asked, still chuckling.

'You can take over on the tiller for a start. Trudi and I have got to skin some chicken breasts for the wedding party this evening and I know you won't want anything to do with that. Let's get moving. The girls are back in business!'

And it was true – they were back in business. At least, the three of them were together and travelling the waterways, cooking up a storm like they'd always done. But there was a shadow hovering in the background. Even though Holme-Lacey wasn't actually with them, sometimes Lia could almost feel his dark, unsmiling face looking over their shoulders.

'Why do we have to wear this clobber?' Jules grumbled one afternoon, changing into the standard waitress's black skirt and little white blouse uniform. 'I mean, does it say anywhere in those Mickey Mouse contracts "Thou shalt not work in jeans and tie-dyed tops"?'

'Loosen up,' Trudi replied. 'Go with the flow for a bit. It won't hurt. And anyway, I think it looks cute with those DMs.'

Jules shot her an unamused look, picked up a tray of asparagus parcels and stomped off across the lawns, slightly awkwardly in her tight pencil skirt and flowery painted boots.

'One of us should catch up with her pretty quick,' Trudi commented, drizzling some olive oil over some sun-dried tomatoes on tiny circles of toast. 'Those Rotarians are the worst. And serving them up asparagus is just asking for trouble . . .'

Lia glanced at her sideways. 'You kidding? There can't be one under sixty.'

Trudi sighed. 'You've still got a lot to learn about men, kiddo. Take it from me: when men get together in these all male clubs, the testosterone level sky rockets. And there are one or two who aren't half bad – for their age. It would only be wasted on Jules.'

'You two aren't sleeping together any more, are you?'

'There are only two cabins. We're still sharing the stern one. You can see that for yourself.'

'You know what I mean.'

'Okay. No. We haven't. Not since Jules came back on board.'

'Is it . . . ? I mean, I know there's still an atmosphere. Even though we have a laugh and pretend it's still the way it was. Under the surface we're all a bit tense.'

'No. I don't think it's business worries knocking the old libido on the head. I think it's 'cause Jules is in love. It was always a risk, wasn't it? One of us falling in love and wanting to settle down. Funny, I always thought it would be you.'

Lia bristled. 'Oh? Because I'm the conventional little straight girl?'

'No – and I'm not one hundred per cent certain you are. But because you're the romantic one.'

Romantic? Lia thought about it for a moment and gave a short, sharp laugh. Maybe in some ways she was. She'd enjoyed imagining Peter as some knight in armour taking all her worries off her shoulders and providing for her. She'd enjoyed his attention, his presents, sipping fine wines barefoot on the croquet lawn on balmy summer evenings with him.

But she wanted more than that, too. She wanted Denny's basic, rough-around-the-edges masculinity and the fact he never tried to tie her down. She wanted Jonathan's curious, kinky vulnerability, his eagerness to act out everything that was wild in her head. And yes, she wanted Trudi's softness, too – her big, warm breasts, her full, questioning lips, her body that knew another woman's sexual responses so well.

'I know I'll never get it all in one package,' she said. 'And that's why there's no danger of me jumping ship.'

'Glad to hear it,' Trudi said and leaned a little closer than was strictly necessary to pick up her tray – close enough for Lia to smell the subtle trace of perfume rising from her neck. 'Now I'd really better catch up with Jules. Check those quiches for me, will you?'

She skipped up out of the hatch and was gone. Lia watched her tanned legs as they disappeared. The ache was still there. The curiosity. Although the flirtiness was often present, neither of them had followed up the unfinished business hanging over from that unexpected morning at the firemen's house.

Lia was beginning to understand why. By tacit, mutual consent they were saving it up. Feeding on the tension. Storing it for a very special night.

The Rotarians' charity garden party was in its dying embers when the call came. Lia was on her way back to the barge, picking at the leftovers on a tray of stuffed baby vegetables, when she saw Jules waving madly and holding out her mobile phone.

'It's him. Reception's pretty crap here, though. You might need to take it the far side of that bridge.'

Lia took the mobile and sprinted down the towpath. She knew full well there was nothing wrong with the reception on the barge. Jules had given her the excuse, though. When she was the other side of the lumbering old brick bridge she stopped and put the phone to her ear. She and Peter were alone now. No one to overhear what she said.

'Hello, Lia?' Peter's suave, cultured tones warmed her like an expensive cognac being swirled in a glass. A voice like that could almost seduce her. Again. 'Are you still all right for next Sunday?'

It was a question he didn't need to ask. Of course they were 'all right' for the following Sunday. It had been written into their strait-jacket contract that they had to go back and cater for any of Peter's private functions – and at cut-throat rates. Clearly he liked having them over a barrel but play-pretended they were willing parties.

'What time will you get here?'

'Early, to set everything up. I know how important this is to you.'

Massage his ego, Lia thought to herself. Men like their egos being stroked as much as their dicks. This particular private function was a gathering of important local business and political contacts. She knew Peter wanted the chance to show off.

'Don't worry,' she finished. 'The menus are sorted. Everything's on order to be delivered to yours. Only our best, most reliable suppliers. We're in control.'

'I'll look forward to seeing you.'

'Good. Are we staying afterwards? After all your important guests have gone away.'

'I can arrange for your old rooms to be made up for you.'

'Oh, Peter, you can do better than that. Hey, just a minute. Are you somewhere where it's difficult to talk?'

'Actually I'm having a meeting with my tax accountant. We're looking at the VAT situation. You know your returns really should be done as part of the group's now.'

Lia chuckled. Knowing Peter was sitting – perhaps in his precious office – across the desk from some strait-laced, serious man who could hear his every word brought out the devil in her. She was going to enjoy winding him up. It was going to be very one-sided. With Peter just a sexy but disembodied voice rather than a taller physical presence, it made her feel, for once, a lot more in control.

'How was Amsterdam? Did you bring me a present this time?'

'Two as a matter of fact.'

'Something to wear? Something I'll like? Something kinky?'

'I think we'll both be pleasantly surprised at the result.'

'I'm glad you brought two. Trudi will feel left out otherwise.'

'Trudi?'

'Yes . . . Peter, I've been having a few thoughts. Next Sunday, after all your respectable guests have gone – they are going afterwards, aren't they?'

'Yes.'

'We could have some fun and games. It's been a long time since I've seen you. Long enough for my imagination to get a little naughty. You said you bought me two presents. To wear for you in bed. Trudi could wear the other one. Only . . . her breasts are so much bigger than mine. I'm sure you'd noticed that.'

'The matter had come to my attention.'

'Whatever you've bought me, if it's in my size, it'll be a tight squeeze for Trudi. Her breasts will be thrusting up out of it like two great globes. Looking like they're really on offer. Do you like the sound of that?'

'Yes – but I'm not sure I see the relevance . . . ?'

Lia looked left and right along the towpath.

There was no one in sight at the moment. She slipped a hand up her petite white blouse and began stroking her breast beneath. She couldn't help getting randy, though that hadn't been the object of the exercise. Hopefully Peter was taking the bait.

'Peter, I know you. When you've just pulled off a successful business gathering you'll be pumping loads of testosterone and as horny as anything. Horny enough to take on two of us. At once. How do you like the sound of that?'

'It sounds an excellent way to round off proceedings.'

Lia squeezed her thighs together under her little black skirt. The temptation to reach down with her free hand and masturbate while she turned Peter on was overwhelming. But she couldn't risk going that far. Not on the very public towpath.

'You sound coy, Peter. Haven't you ever had a threesome before? I have. And Trudi's had dozens. Don't worry. We know just what to do. Does the thought of two women together arouse you? Trudi and I will dress up in whatever you've bought us. We'll all go to your room. You can just lie on that big bed if you like, and watch us undress each other. Don't forget, Trudi's breasts will be straining to get out of their cups. Can you imagine that? Can you imagine how grateful they'll be when I undo all the hooks and buttons and let them spill softly out into my hands? And then I'll kiss them better – all over those fantastic curves and coffee-coloured nipples. Did you know Trudi has really prominent, dark nipples? And they're fantastically responsive when you flick your tongue backwards and forwards all over them. Are you hard yet, Peter?'

'I can confirm that.'

'And I bet your accountant's still sitting there looking at you. You'd love to reach down, undo your flies and rub your dick, wouldn't you? But you can't. Is it driving you crazy?'

'Incredibly. But do go on to explain your plan.'

'You'd better make sure you have some of that fabulous lotion handy. You know – the one you used when you took me up the arse. Trudi and I will smother the fronts of our bodies with it and writhe up and down against each other. You'll see our breasts bob and bounce all over the place. How close to coming do you think you'll be by then?'

'It's becoming an urgent consideration right now.'

Lia grinned. She squeezed her own nipple tighter. If only she were doing this somewhere private and safe. Why the hell hadn't she thought of that? She was going crazy for release. And yet that tension added to the spice.

'Then Trudi will kiss her way down my body. She's amazing when she does that. Oh yes, we've tried it. Did you think we hadn't, all cooped up on the barge like that? I'll lie back and sigh. She'll poke out her long tongue to pleasure my pussy. She's so good at that. And that's the point – you won't be able to stand it any longer . . .'

'Go on.'

'How hard is your dick now, Peter? Really making a big bulge in your pin-striped suit? I hope you don't have to stand up to shake your accountant's hand when he leaves. He'll wonder what on earth you've been thinking about during your meeting. Because it won't go down of its own accord – will it – a hard on like that.'

'Go on – what you were saying before . . .'

'Oh yes. Sorry. Didn't mean to tease you, Peter. You won't be able to stand it any longer and you'll leap up from the bed. Your cock will be standing out like a great, thick lance. You'll drag Trudi aside and plunge your big dick into me instead. I'll gasp with pleasure. I hadn't been expecting anything so meaty. You'll thrust into me so fast and wild and sure you'll take me to heaven, like you always do . . .'

She trailed off, sighing. It was a genuine sigh, not part of the act. She'd got herself so aroused by now she was aching to feel his cock stretching her sex.

'But it won't end there, Peter. You'll be feeling so bullish with two women in your bed. You've always thought Trudi a bit uppity, haven't you? I'll let you into a secret. She is. She needs teaching a lesson. A little humiliation. I'll help you. I'll hold her down for you while you spank her round, pert arse. That's a sweet, creamy coffee colour, too. Honestly, I know. It'll jiggle while you're spanking it. And she'll be crying out for mercy. You'll be getting turned on again, just having her in your power. The blood will be pumping and pumping back into your cock, it'll be standing up and wobbling as you give her a good hard spank. What will you do then, Peter? Will you pour some more body lotion down between her cheeks and take her by the back door, or will you make her go down on her knees before you and suck your cock?'

'Either possibility is worth exploring.'

'Think about it. Think about it hard. On Sunday we'll make it all come true.'

Abruptly Lia cut the connection and pressed the

phone against her chest, against her racing heart. She was desperate for some release herself. And she was more than a little apprehensive about the train of fantasy she'd set in motion.

She walked briskly back to the barge. Her sex was buzzing. Oh, to hell with waiting for that special night. If Trudi was in a remotely frisky mood, she wanted to get laid.

Trudi had other things on her mind, though. She was sitting at the galley table, waiting for Lia with a pot of coffee and drumming two fingers against her front teeth.

'Marlene,' she said when Lia had sat down. 'We've got to think of something to get that one out of the way.'

CHAPTER

10

A fter some local dignitary's fiftieth birthday party, an exhibition of canal history and an open-air classical concert where Jules stuffed shredded paper napkins in her ears, they were ready to head back to Peter Holme-Lacey's.

It was the first time they'd approached the house from the river. It looked different from this angle, Lia thought. More benign. As the house came into view – slowly, at the walking pace of the barge – rising over the trees and the slight hill she hadn't noticed before, the old red bricks had a warm glow in the early-morning August sunshine. It hardly seemed the same place where she'd felt trapped.

But it wasn't just the illusion of seeing the mansion in a different way. This time they were arriving under their own steam and on their terms. It made a difference. Lia felt the power quicken in her as she tied up the *Lady Jayne*, took a deep breath and gazed uphill towards the house. And power was sexy.

It was still early when they let themselves in by the mansion's back door. No one seemed to be about. Was Peter avoiding them? Was he saving a face-to-face meeting for the promised finale?

They got to work. It was what they were good at. In the kitchens the supplies they'd ordered had arrived properly labelled and everything was as it should be. They began unpacking, defrosting, peeling, chopping and skinning. No one said much – but it wasn't a tense silence. There was a sly, suppressed excitement in the way they worked and they often caught each other smiling with sideways glances.

By midday, Peter's expensively dressed guests were arriving and sampling the drinks Jules and Trudi carried in on trays. Lia stayed in the kitchen. She wanted to keep out of Peter's way for the moment. Let him wonder. Let him wait. He wouldn't come looking for her, she knew that. They were both playing a needling, waiting game. It tightened the knot of anticipation just below her solar plexus.

'How's things?' she asked Trudi, who'd come back into the kitchen for the large plate of salmon mousse.

'Great. We're a hit with the punters – anyone can see that. Even old Holme-Lacey looks pleased with us.'

'How's things with him? How does he look?'

'If you're pining, you can go see for yourself.'

'I am *not*! We agreed this was the way to keep him on his toes.'

'I know – just couldn't resist it. If you really want to know, though, he looks good in that cream linen suit. Not all blokes could carry it off. Needs a good body underneath – which I'm guessing he has. Won't have to guess much longer, eh?'

Trudi winked as she negotiated the door, balancing the tray of salmon on her curvy hip and holding a jug of tangy lemon dressing in the other hand. Lia took in a sharp breath. Peter wasn't the only thing tightening the knot in her stomach.

The afternoon shadows lengthened on the back lawn as guests wandered there, swirling liqueurs in their hands. Many were tempted by just one more of the summer-fruit-filled meringue nests that Jules was carrying. She came back to the kitchen, licking cream off her fingers like a cat. 'Time to make that call,' she said, took out her mobile and disappeared into the store room next door.

Eventually Trudi came back with trayfulls of empty glasses. 'At last – they're beginning to make a move. Let's get the boring stuff out of the way, then we can party on!' She began loading the dishwasher. 'I'm getting excited, tell you the truth. I haven't been laid since . . . Ah, that reminds me.' She skipped over to the meat freezer with a typical Trudi, unselfconscious shimmy. Then she wedged open the freezer door with a stray piece of packaging. 'That should get the temperatures looking nice and illegal in time for Paul's next inspection visit. Just another spanner in the works. Every little helps.'

The mansion was quiet by the time Lia ventured down the oak-panelled hall. It had a peaceful air, the way a building can only when it has so much history behind it. It had seemed a safe place once. Could it still be? Was she about to make a big mistake?

'Lia?' She recognised the voice. A low, sexy voice with a wicked edge that tugged all the right strings inside her. It could divert her, given half the chance. She turned.

'You're looking fantastic,' Peter continued. 'I missed seeing you earlier. You haven't gone all shy on me? Especially after that rather naughty phone call . . .'

He moved closer and took her in his arms, tightening his grip around her.

'I was busy in the kitchen,' she replied into his shoulder. 'Business before pleasure. I had to make sure everything went perfectly.'

'And you did. I really appreciate it, Lia. I've never been sure of your colleagues, but I know you,' he tipped her face up to meet his, 'and I understand each other.'

He kissed her, forcing his tongue into her mouth. She emptied her head of everything and just enjoyed the warmth and friction of his body writhing in a sensitive part of hers. He might be an arrogant bastard, but he turned her on.

'You've fed us so well this afternoon,' he murmured, breaking off, 'I'm not sure I need anything else before bed time. And I know I said you looked fantastic in your waitress stuff, but not as fantastic as you'll look in what I brought you back from Amsterdam. Shall we . . . ?'

'Wait.'

He did a double-take. When Peter made a suggestion he expected her to treat it as a command.

'I was serious about Trudi joining us,' Lia continued.

Peter moved his jaw from side to side a few

times as if he was thinking. She knew he hated being taken off guard. And she was listening hard for the sound of a motorbike engine approaching down the long drive.

'Go upstairs,' she said, 'and wait for us. I know you like to get ready.'

Peter looked once or twice over his shoulder – but didn't say anything – as he walked away down the dim, quiet hall towards the stairs. Lia grinned to herself but hid her grin by turning away. Usually Peter Holme-Lacey never looked back.

Just as she heard his heavy footfalls fading away, motorbike tyres crunched to a halt on the gravel outside. Jules came running from the kitchen.

Lynne swung off the motorbike and removed her helmet. Lia could see a flash of dark uniform showing under the collar of her biking leathers.

'Present from Jonathan,' she said, tossing Lia a small rucksack. It clanked as Lia caught it. Then she turned to Jules. 'Right, babe. Where d'you want me?'

Trudi had arrived now and was standing beside Lia. She was fingering the neckline of her tight waitress's blouse – perhaps unconsciously – giving little flashes of the deep, warm, café au lait cleavage beneath. Lia became very aware of Trudi's towering height so close to her. It was like standing next to a man she had unfinished business with.

Jules winked and gave them a thumbs up. Then she and Lynne turned and disappeared into the too-silent house.

'Just you and me, kiddo,' Trudi murmured. Lia noticed her fiddling had made the top button come loose and more of that gaze-drawing cleavage was evident. You just couldn't help looking. Lia suspected that even a 100 per cent straight woman wouldn't be able to resist a peek. 'Ready?'

'As I'll ever be.'

They turned and went back in. As they mounted the long staircase Trudi gave her hand a squeeze.

Peter wasn't in his bedroom. For a moment that threw Lia. But she could feel his presence – something subtler than a sound or a shadow – and she realised he must be in the en suite bathroom, waiting and keeping his breathing quiet. She put her finger to her lips and inclined her head towards the bathroom door. Trudi understood.

Lia put Jonathan's rucksack down slowly, quietly and tucked it out of sight beside the bed. Then she saw the lingerie that was spread out on the duvet ready for them.

One was a fairly conventional basque – stiff scarlet material overlaid with spidery black lace. She could just imagine the 'bad girl' from some old western movie wearing it, probably with a black choker and tall feathers in her hair. Lia picked it up and pressed the fabric into the semblance of a waist. The material was resistant, restraining. What would it feel like on?

'That's got your name on it,' Trudi whispered in her ear. 'Sexy but classy. Try it on. I'll help. Remember how I love dressing you up?'

Lia tapped her finger against her lip once more. She didn't want Trudi giving the game away about that episode. Peter still believed in Miranda: Denny said he'd phoned the pub asking to speak to her again. And no doubt Peter had his ear pressed against the bathroom door right now.

Trudi chuckled as if she'd got the hint. Then she

picked up the other outfit and held it against her. 'Whereas this is all mine. Pure "what you see is what you get" tartiness.'

It was a tight, wet-look, black body that came up high at the throat. But there was a cut-away panel around the navel, perfect for showing off Trudi's glittering jewel. More than that, the cups were totally open. Trudi's big breasts would be fully on display.

'Yes, you'd better wear that one,' Lia replied, getting into the mood for this. 'If you wore something he'd bought for my cup size you'd be squashed.'

'So, we going to help each other get into them?' Trudi was already undoing the rest of the buttons down the front of her figure-hugging blouse. Underneath she was wearing a deep plunge, push-up bra. Not that her fabulous breasts needed emphasis. As the blouse fell fully open, Lia felt those instincts she'd repressed for so long come into their own.

She pulled Trudi close and slipped the blouse from her shoulders. As she stood on tiptoes and kissed Trudi's full, warm lips she ran her hands over her friend's breasts, feeling their weight in her palms. Friend and lover. She could say that now.

After fumbling against Trudi's back for a moment or two she walked her fingers round and found the catch of the deep plunge bra nestling between her breasts. Lia undid it, one handed. Trudi's breasts bobbed into her welcoming hands.

'Talk to me,' Trudi whispered in her ear. 'Talk dirty. And loud. We need to buy time.'

They drew back and looked at each other for a moment. They both knew Peter was listening at the door. From the almost imperceptible creak, Lia wondered if he'd opened it a crack and was watching them through the gap in the hinges. But this wasn't about Peter any more or turning the tables. This was about the need she felt for Trudi's enticing flesh.

'Your turn,' Lia said. For a moment she felt awkward. Phone sex was one thing but talking dirty with another woman when your audience was a few metres away? She heard her voice crackle with the newness of it. 'Undo my blouse. Set me free.'

'You want to rub our tits together? Fantastic. Let's hope Peter left some of that famous body lotion handy so we can slip over and under each other like naughty seals.'

There was something about Trudi's strident South African accent. It carried even when she wasn't trying. They grinned impishly at each other as Trudi unbuttoned Lia's blouse and there was a creak like antique hinges being eased back another fraction.

'You've got beautiful breasts, Lia,' Trudi said as she slipped off her bra. 'So pert. That classic half-grapefruit shape. So good to hold. And they look great without a bra under a silky T-shirt. I've been watching. You know I love to watch you move around the boat.'

'There's that body lotion. On the cabinet. Let's rub it all over each other and dance up close.'

'Patience. Let's take our skirts off first.' Trudi's hand was on Lia's zip. As she eased it down her other hand fondled Lia's buttocks, slipping the skirt down over her hips and sneaking her fingers inside Lia's stretch-lace panties. 'You've got a gorgeous arse, too. All curvy and womanly but taut. And smooth. So baby soft. I could feel your arse all day.'

'Don't. You'd drive me too crazy.' Lia was easing down Trudi's skirt. She wasn't surprised to find Trudi hadn't bothered with underwear. 'I'd want to get on to the main action.' She writhed in Trudi's arms, taken aback by her genuine strength. But when she finally wriggled free and reached for the body lotion, Trudi held her back.

'Let's not get sticky just yet. Time to play dressing-up games. I'll hook your basque up at the back. No – turn round. Wouldn't want just anyone to get an eyeful . . .'

Trudi settled Lia's breasts into the basque's stiff cups. They teetered precariously in their lacy confines: if she breathed too deeply her nipples rose like twin suns momentarily over the wispy trim.

When the basque was fully hooked up, Lia realised how tight Trudi had made it. She'd never felt this constricted before. But the constriction – the pressure on her stomach, the awareness of her tight, clinched-in waist was its own kind of pleasure. The pressure made her sensitive to stirrings in her womb: that deepest seat of female need. She fel a little light-headed with the shallower breaths she was forced to take.

She turned round slowly so Trudi could see the effect.

'Fantastic, Li. Gives you a real hourglass figure. I reckon those black stockings on the bed were meant for you. Aren't they so sheer? As if just breathing on them would ladder them . . .' Trudi trailed off. Lia felt a shiver run through her as she let the 'breathing' image run through her head and was delighted how wicked she found the idea of Trudi breathing on her stocking-clad legs. 'And that tiny little scrap of a lacy G-string,' Trudi continued, 'must be yours as well. Shame to hide the most delicious part of you away. Slip it on. I don't need one. This thing's got an easy-access crotch.' She held up her wet-look costume and wiggled two fingers through the gap to prove it. 'He must have been having some real horny thoughts when he chose this. I'll bet his cock was right up hard inside his pants.'

They winked at each other. Both had heard another creak behind the bathroom door as if someone were shifting his weight on old floor-boards.

'Here,' Trudi began again, holding up the black body stocking. 'Help me with this. It's so tight. We'll have to squeeze.'

Lia helped her. The wet-look material was stretched so tight across Trudi's back and buttocks it gleamed. The top was a kind of halter neck arrangement, which lifted Trudi's voluptuous breasts but at the same time left them totally bare. With the black material surrounding them – above, below, between – they seemed more visible, more in-your-face than if she'd been naked.

'They look like they're begging to be touched,' Lia whispered – and it wasn't just part of the game to wind Peter up. She was saying the first things that came into her head.

'Don't make them beg, then.' Trudi took her hand. 'Let's lie down and have some fun.'

They sank down together on the wide double bed. Trudi pulled Lia towards her with genuine, irresistible strength. Their lips met and fastened ardently on each other. Trudi's mouth felt as pillowy and sensual as Lia remembered. Their lips parted at the same moment and their tongues writhed and danced. How long they spent kissing Lia couldn't tell. Time seemed to dissolve as Trudi's tongue explored her space. But there was a rising heat tightening up her sex. She couldn't ignore it any longer. She needed to move things up a gear.

Lia eased herself back from Trudi's clingy mouth. She slid down her friend's magnificent body a little way and buried her face between her big, proud breasts. At the same time she slipped astride one of Trudi's muscular, athletic thighs. Trudi caught the hint and brought her thigh hard up between Lia's legs. She rocked her pelvis in a slow figure of eight, grinding her yearning clitoris against Trudi's tense quad muscles. Beneath her on the bed, Trudi thrust her pubis up to meet her. They were really getting each other's pussies worked up now.

Lia opened her mouth and took one of Trudi's outrageously erectile nipples deep inside. She teased it with her tongue. The dark coffee nipple peaked even further, lengthening and responding in her mouth as if she were sucking a tiny, tiny cock. And Trudi moaned in pleasure as loud as any man. Louder, even, and more joyfully. Her cries sent shivers of response through Lia. Nothing else mattered at this moment, just the fact she was giving such erotic pleasure to someone she loved so much.

The playground of another woman's breasts was something she'd never fully appreciated – not even in that quick early-morning fumble at the firemen's house. She took her time now. She kissed her way over their yielding slopes and buried her face in that deep but firm cleavage. Trudi's spicy scent was particularly rich there. She kissed and licked her way up the other side and took the nipple she hadn't yet sucked deep in her mouth. She drew on it hard, even tightening her teeth ever so gently around it at one point. Trudi yelped but the cry was of intense pleasure, not pain. Lia closed her hand round the other warm, proud breast and began rolling the very point of Trudi's nipple like a marble between her finger and thumb.

'You've got me so horny,' Trudi whispered, and Lia knew it wasn't fake. 'I'm so close to coming. If only you had a cock and fucked me right now I think I'd come on the spot.'

Lia's mouth was deliciously full. She didn't want to relinquish sucking Trudi's responsive, rubbery nipple in order to reply. But the thought was going round her head: I'm not sure I ever want another cock. All your sexy warmth and womanliness is in danger of converting me . . .

And then the door creaked. Trudi's body tensed beneath her. They'd almost forgotten about Peter watching them.

Lia turned her head just a little. She didn't want to stop what she was doing. She poked her tongue out as far as it would go and kept on flicking Trudi's nipple with the very tip as she tilted her head and looked sideways at the figure in the bathroom doorway.

Peter was wearing his expensive silk dressing gown. But he'd let it fall open. Jutting out through the opening was the highest, most swollen erection Lia had ever seen him sport.

He let the dressing gown fall from his shoulders and walked slowly over towards the bed without saying anything.

'Lia was right,' Trudi murmured, wriggling her way out from under. 'Those abs are in fantastic shape. In fact, pretty fantastic shape all over.'

Lia felt sidelined. A stab of jealousy went through her. A stab of anger. She rolled to one side and took a deep breath to get the anger under control. There's a plan, she reminded herself, don't blow it. Keep on track. Use that jealousy.

Because it was true – strong emotions were part of the same thing. Jealousy stirred like a snake in Lia's lower belly, stirring the desire that had already risen. And the tightness of the basque pinching in her stomach seemed to focus it all there.

'Come and join us.' Lia edged away from Trudi and patted the space that had opened, reluctantly, between them. 'See, we saved you a place.'

Peter still said nothing. That wasn't like him, Lia thought. Peter was never lost for the controlling word. But right now he wasn't in control. And keeping quiet avoided admitting it.

He eased his way in between them. Lia tried not to stare at his erection. It was in danger of distracting her – perhaps she wasn't ready to give up the joys of a good, firm, male organ just yet! Trudi propped herself up on one arm to dominate Peter. This was going to be the tricky bit.

It had to go just right. They weren't going to get a second chance. Trudi was incredibly strong for a woman and Lia knew she was in pretty good shape herself after a year of handling the boat. But

Peter worked out, too. This had to be perfectly timed. As Trudi began talking in her throaty, sexy voice, Lia wriggled to the side of the bed. The stiff basque made it awkward.

'Bet you've wanted this for ages,' Trudi began, moving on to all fours to straddle Peter. 'An eyeful of my tits, I mean. Well, now's your chance. I'm going to drape them all over your face. And you know what? Men tell me this feels even better if they close their eyes and just let me dangle them all over their eyelids, noses, lips ... Yeah, that's right ...'

Trudi had her large hands clamped on Peter's forearms, Lia noticed. Good. She was holding tight. And he was obviously well away with the sensation of her bullet-hard nipples grazing his face. The time was right.

She ducked down and groped for the rucksack she'd stowed under the bed. She raised it ever so carefully so the contents didn't clank. While Trudi was swaying her pendant breasts backwards and forwards over Peter's grinning face, Lia locked one end of each set of handcuffs to the chunky wooden uprights at the four corners of the bed. She was so precise there was only the barest click.

Trudi turned to her and nodded. Her eyes flashed wide open for 'Now!' She reached for one set of wrist restraints; Lia grabbed the other. In a simultaneous movement they locked the distracted Peter tight.

When he realised what had happened, Peter grunted and tried to sit up. Even if Trudi hadn't still been sitting astride him, weighing him down, they hadn't left him enough slack. The chains clinked but didn't give.

'We changed the script,' Trudi told him. She was kneeling upright now, still astride him and with her pussy lips, in their open-crotched body stocking, just millimetres above his straining cock. She was still swaying her hips a little and her provocative breasts were jiggling in time. Peter couldn't keep his eyes off them. Lia took advantage of his submissiveness and dived to the foot of the bed to fasten his ankle restraints. Their prey was helpless as Trudi continued, 'You've never been trussed up and dominated by women before? Thought not. Well, relax and enjoy . . .'

Peter shrugged – or tried to shrug with his arms pinioned up and above him. 'I'm prepared to have my horizons broadened,' he said with a smile, but his voice lacked its usual aplomb.

Trudi moved backwards. Peter was looking increasingly hopeful. Perhaps, Lia thought, he assumed she was getting into position to lay herself down and suck his cock. But Trudi moved back far out of contact with his supine body and rested her arse against the carved rail at the foot of the bed.

'C'mon, Li. Let's start loving each other up like before we got interrupted. Oh, sorry, Peter – was there some misunderstanding? Did you think we were going to crawl all over you and rub our bodies up against you and maybe slap you around just a little bit while you were chained up like that? No. When I said "dominate" perhaps I should have said "humiliate". We're going to show you that you don't matter as much as you think you do . . .'

Lia moved round to stand behind Trudi who was poised against the footrail, her firm, trained muscles holding her like some trapeze artist about to take flight. Just behind her on an antique set of drawers was the bottle of cocoa butter body lotion, casually placed. Peter's doing? Lia picked up the bottle and tipped generous dollops into both palms. Then she cupped Trudi's breasts in the sinfully smooth lotion.

Trudi gasped. The lotion must have been cool against her desire-hot breasts. Lia could feel her nipples tightening into peaks with the contrary sensations of cold and arousal. As her hands roved, warming up the lotion and making it runnier, more slippery, Lia heard Trudi moan in unambiguous pleasure.

As the cocoa butter spread out across those big, coffee-cream breasts they became disobedient in Lia's hands. They slipped out of her grasp, bouncing with a life of their own. The effect on Peter was obvious torture. Lia rested her chin on Trudi's shoulder to watch him writhing on the bed. His cock was so stretched, touching his navel, she could see the skin gleaming under the strain and every vein taut. His forearms were tensed as if his most immediate need was to get one hand free, grab his cock and give himself some relief. But there wasn't going to be any relief. Not yet. The girls had him where they wanted him and they were going to take their time.

Lia relinquished one of Trudi's heavy breasts and let her hand trail moistly down over the wet-look fabric. It had its own sensual appeal. So very touchable. Once Lia had felt it, she had to keep on feeling, stroking, exploring. It was easy to see how fetishists got started.

Her fingers came to rest around Trudi's navel

and the cut-out panel that showed off her tight, perfect belly. Today she was wearing a belly bar, which dangled streams of red and clear diamante sparkles. If Trudi swayed her hips they swayed seductively in time. The sunlight through the window was low now (the time? Lia had no idea) but one or two of the stones caught the light as they danced over her lower belly. Lia saw Peter's gaze flicker down to the swinging jewels, signposting the way to treasure even lower down.

But for the moment Lia kept her lotion-slippery finger circling Trudi's belly button. She knew her friend found this such a sensual caress. And the novelty of toying with that body piercing fascinated her. She slipped the steel bar backwards and forwards in Trudi's flesh a millimetre or so, then felt braver and played with it as far as it would go. Trudi sighed, relaxed back against her and shivered with a particular kind of sensual pleasure Lia tried hard to imagine.

Trudi hoisted her arse fully up on to the carved rail and spread her legs wide. The crotch-opening gaped and, from the way Peter's eyes widened, her juicy sex must have been fully on display. Lia had never actually seen Trudi's pussy lips close up. Were they as outrageously dark as her nipples? Lia walked her fingers lower down and touched her friend's sex. It was warm and slippery and didn't need any cocoa butter. She flexed her wrist and sank two fingers deep inside. She still she didn't know what it looked like.

Lia grinned. Peter was fascinated: his face was a picture – as open-mouthed and incredulous as a boy's. Trudi spread her legs as wide as they would go, leaning her weight back against Lia a little more. Lia envied him. Helpless as he was, he was getting the most amazing, sexy, no-holds-barred view of a woman's most intimate part being pleasured by another woman.

Lia slipped her fingers in and out of Trudi's sex, keeping the pad of her thumb pressed against her clitoris. Her other hand switched backwards and forwards between Trudi's thrusting breasts, keeping them both pleasured. Trudi writhed against her in ecstasy. It was difficult keeping their balance like that. Lia held her breath – she knew how wild and uninhibited Trudi could be when she came. A moment later Trudi froze and cried out as she climaxed, her vaginal muscles clasping sweetly round Lia's two fingers as her orgasm blossomed then died away.

Lia burrowed deeper into Trudi. She knew she loved a full penetration in the afterglow of orgasm – but how many men could understand that? Trudi relaxed against Lia's shoulder and sighed deeply in appreciation of her gentle, probing afterplay. When finally Lia slipped her hand out, Trudi pressed Lia's fingers to her lips and kissed them, clearly relishing the perfume of her own musky sweet juices.

'Thank you,' she said between kisses. 'Your fingers are amazing. What more could we want? Unless . . . Let's see what other presents our kinky friend has sent us.'

Trudi swung gracefully down off the footrail. Lia touched the dimmer switch to subtly illuminate the scene; the daylight outside had gone completely now. Trudi hunted in the rucksack beside the bed. She grinned as she pulled something out. Lia was intrigued. *That* hadn't been on the shopping list they'd texted Jonathan.

Trudi cradled the double-ended dildo against her body. Each prong was fatter and longer than Peter's erection and Trudi was clearly enjoying displaying it to him. Lia glanced down and saw his cock seemed to have lolled slightly to one side.

Trudi looked back at Lia. 'Shall we have some fun with this? Why not get on all fours and I'll take you from behind like I was a real bullish stud.'

Lia crawled on to the bed. It was a big, big bed and there was room for her to prowl like a cat in the space below Peter's splayed out legs. The very act of going on all fours made her breasts spill out of the wispy basque cups. Peter was staring at them. His erection raised its head proudly again.

Behind her, Lia heard Trudi's, 'Mmm,' as she slipped one prong of the dildo into her juiced-up pussy and then the sounds of buckles as Trudi pulled the straps tight. The mattress bounced as Trudi climbed on behind her. Then she felt her friend peel down the wispy G-string and fondle her buttocks.

Trudi slipped a forefinger into Lia's sex. 'You ready?' she whispered. 'You feel ready.'

'Yeah.'

'You better be horny. 'Cause I've been a real mate and given you the bigger end. When I slip this monster into you it's going to feel like no fuck you've ever had.' She made an exaggerated show of looking over Lia's shoulder. 'And certainly no fuck you've ever had from him.'

That was part of the play acting. Lia knew it. Peter's erection was looking as impressive as ever, despite all this time and no prospect of release. He must be going crazy for someone to touch it. He lifted his gaze from her spilling-out breasts and met her eyes, but she looked back without mercy.

And then Trudi penetrated her. Lia gasped involuntarily as she did. The dildo felt monumental as it slipped in. It stretched her far more than she was used to being stretched. It was as if all her prayers for a sensitive man with a massive cock had been answered. There was no pressure on her clitoris but for once that didn't matter. The huge dildo felt like the most well-endowed of her lovers when on the point of coming. But this was capable of going on for ever – and it was stimulating all the right spots inside.

Trudi reached round and tweaked Lia's nipples, which had escaped from their lacy binding. 'Beautiful, aren't they?' she said for Peter's benefit. 'All peachy-ripe and pert. But I'm sure you know that. I'm sure you know what they feel like in your hands. I'll bet you're going mad to touch them now.'

Trudi continued to fondle Lia's bare breasts while she thrust – tiny, controlled thrusts. Anything wilder with the size of that dildo would just have been too much. Lia was on the way to coming now. Trudi was pleasuring her selflessly and the pleasure was the whole centre of her being.

Then she made the mistake of looking straight at Peter for just a split second. He met her gaze and mouthed, 'Please.'

She couldn't remember him ever saying that before. And the hunger in his eyes was so genuine. He'd been her lover. She'd shared this very bed with him. He'd opened her up to games she'd never dared before. Just as he mouthed 'please' a second time, she bent her elbows, eased forwards and down and began kissing the tip of his quivering cock.

In doing so, Trudi's hands slipped away from her breasts. They just wouldn't reach in this position. But the meatiness of Peter's cock against her lips felt so good. And she began rubbing her breasts against his thighs instead. Between the hairiness of his legs and the scratchiness of the lace cups, which had ridden up over her nipples again, her sensitive peaks were getting the stimulation they loved.

Lia turned her attention fully to Peter's straining prick. As she ran her tongue along its shiny underside he shuddered and groaned. Having this much power over him felt sexy. And yet she loved giving his body satisfaction, too. And what had they intended to happen? It wasn't as if they really had a script. And they were all meant to enjoy it, after all. Forget it, her sensual side told her: forget anything that's going to happen later, outside of this room. Just go with the flow and do what feels good.

And right now, flicking her tongue along the iron-bar underside of his shaft felt very, very good. The only thing that felt better was easing her body forwards a little more, mouthing the yielding cap of his foreskin and then engulfing his entire cock in her warm mouth. She could feel his blood pulsing against the stretched corners of her lips. Peter was close to coming in her mouth.

Trudi had given a little grunt as Lia had begun to suck Peter off. Disapproval? Lia wasn't quite sure. Perhaps she thought she'd given in too easily. But Trudi kept thrusting the dildo into her with absolute precision, absolute skill. While her hands could no longer reach Lia's breasts, she moved one back and began toying with Lia's clitoris instead. Lia gave a muffled moan – it would have been much louder if she hadn't been gagged by the fatness of Peter's cock. Everything was being pleasured at once. Her body was in heaven.

She felt Trudi's finger so acutely as it drew tiny circles on her moist, slippery clitoris. Her hungry sex felt divinely stretched. She only had to shimmy her breasts against Peter's muscular thighs for her nipples to feel everything they needed to. With all this pleasure coming to her at once, her tongue on Peter's cock had become lazy. But he hardly needed it. It must have been driving him crazy with frustration but she could feel the tension building in his prick.

Trudi pressed just a little harder and that tipped her over the edge. In this strange, stretched position her orgasm seemed to hang in the balance a moment before sweeping up through the centre of her body. She gave a stifled moan as she came. Her mouth tightened round Peter's cock. His captive body tensed and he climaxed copiously in her mouth.

Lia raised herself up, away from his body. Trudi withdrew the dildo and behind her Lia could hear a sound like unbuckling straps.

'I hope you've got something in reserve,' Trudi said, cuddling close behind Lia and looking down over her shoulder at the helpless Peter. 'Because we haven't finished yet. Not by a long shot. It's like that with us girls. Dare you to keep up!'

With that, she glided her hands down over the front of Lia's stiff lace basque and began unclipping the suspender straps. When the stockings were sliding down under their own whispery weight Trudi moved her hands up and round again. Her touch wasn't just a functional thing. Whatever she was doing, she moved with sensuality. Lia felt her skin alive, her nerve endings dancing under Trudi's long, tapping fingers.

Trudi began unhooking the back of Lia's basque. In another moment it slipped down and Lia was fully naked. She turned to Trudi and wrapped her arms around her, kissing her deeply all the while as she reached up behind to unzip the wet-look bodysuit.

Trudi pulled back, reluctantly, from their hungry French kiss. 'Leave it on. I kinda like the feeling . . . And you know you can get to all the best bits.'

She was right Lia thought as she began kissing her way down over Trudi's voluptuous body. All the best bits. That was the thing about Trudi. No false modesty. Her absolute confidence in her body was like a sexual magnet.

She kissed her way over the billowing domes of Trudi's breasts. The contrast between their welcoming softness and the severe black fabric was a sexy shock. Lia took Trudi's prominent nipples in her mouth, sucked hard, sucked furiously and Trudi moaned. Neither of them spared a look for Peter, supine on the bed below them. Lia thought about him, though, as she flicked the very tips of Trudi's nipples and made them peak like little missiles. Would he get hard again watching their lesbian pleasuring?

Trudi was still kneeling up high. Lia knelt down as low as she could, her bare arse poked towards Peter's face, and began tonguing Trudi's belly button through the body stocking's cunningly cut-out panel.

The body bar fascinated her, particularly the gleaming silvery ball above the navel itself, anchoring the piercing into Trudi's toned, smooth abdomen. Lia circled the tiny ball with the tip of her tongue. It was unfamiliar, unyielding and bobbly against the packed nerve endings of her tongue. The effect on Trudi was unmistakable. She writhed her hips before Lia's face and sighed with pleasure.

Lia had gone as low as she could in that position. She pulled back for a moment. 'Lie down,' she said softly, 'and what I was just doing to the end of your body bar I'm going to do to your clit.'

She heard her voice sound curiously confident as she said it – sexy and in control. More in control than she felt. She'd never tongued another woman's pussy. It was the last taboo. A line she was nervous to cross.

But Trudi was already lying down crossways on the wide bed. She was spreading her legs wide, inviting Lia in. The body suit's crotch-opening gaped, giving an intimate view of Trudi's dark, purplish lower lips. Lia gave a quick glance to her left before she went down.

Peter was hard again. He was craning his neck desperately to get a good view of what they were doing. Lia almost chuckled as she moved into position between Trudi's fantastic muscular thighs. She'd never understand why men got so horny watching two women fuck. But right now she wasn't complaining.

Trudi flexed her thighs a little and wriggled her hips. She was clearly getting impatient for things to start. Lia dipped her head and kissed those wisps of Trudi's black, crinkly bush that were showing through the crotch opening.

They had their own, musky scent. And their own springy, soft texture, too. For a moment Lia regretted that Trudi wasn't completely naked so she could comb the tip of her nose through that luxuriant hair over and over, her quick breaths sending Trudi wild. But there would be other chances . . .

She moved lower and began kissing circles around Trudi's moist clitoris. For a split second she glanced up and saw Trudi enthusiastically fondling her own proud breasts. Trust her! She wasn't in the least inhibited about this.

Lia ran her tongue up and down Trudi's soft, fleshy groove. The clear, fresh juices were plentiful. A professional caterer, Lia was accustomed to tasting sauces on the tip of her tongue, rolling them round her mouth to get the full effect. Trudi's juices were no different. On the tip and edges of her tongue they were salty – but subtly so. As she tasted them more fully with the whole of her mouth there was something else: the nearest she could come to defining it was 'lemony'. Why ever had she been so nervous of another woman's honey? Now she dipped her tongue more fully in the pot.

Trudi squirmed as Lia penetrated her orally as fully as she could. While she couldn't rival the hugeness of a cock or a dildo, Lia knew she could wriggle her prehensile tongue inside her friend, and that would be a feeling like no other. She was an expert at receiving cunnilingus. She knew what she loved men to do to her. Now she did it all for Trudi. She held nothing back.

Trudi gasped with pleasure and bucked her

hips. Lia clasped them to try and stay with her. She knew how horny Trudi could get. She knew it wouldn't take her long to come. Trudi's moans were getting louder and, in another quickly snatched glance, Lia saw she was rolling both her nipples tightly between thumbs and forefingers bringing herself closer to the brink.

Lia flicked her tongue up and down over Trudi's hard clitoris. It was the lightest of flickers, though. It kept Trudi hanging on the edge of orgasm for just a few moments longer, just a few more moments to build up the aching longing and the tension. Trudi was making a little grunting noise deep in her throat from pleasure and impatience mixed and then she gave the loud cry Lia had come to recognise. Quickly she pressed her mouth as tight as she could against Trudi's quim to feel her whole sex pulse with orgasm.

Slowly, slowly they raised themselves up. Lia extended her hand and pulled Trudi to a sitting position. It was a tender handclasp. They didn't say anything but held hands longer than they needed to. Trudi's fingers felt so strong against hers. So capable.

Peter moaned, clanking his restraints as he strained. It was as if he feared they'd forgotten him in their mutual pleasure. Being by-passed was one thing he couldn't stand.

Trudi grinned and turned to him. 'Did you enjoy that, too? By the look of your cock I reckon you did.' She reached over and stroked it up and down – just once. Peter shuddered. 'Hmm, hard as a rod again. Maybe you might be some use to us after all.'

She turned and looked at Lia. This was the part

they'd avoided discussing. Full penetration. And who was going to mount him? Lia had felt his cock in her so many times. She quite understood if the greedy Trudi was curious. And yet ... She and Peter had a history – of sorts. That jealousy snake shivered deep in her belly again.

Trudi murmured softly, 'Lia, he's all yours.'

Lia positioned herself astride Peter's body. Their eyes met and he smiled at her. That smile was dangerous, but it was probably too late to do anything now, anyway. She smiled, too, but she looked quickly down at his straining cock.

At her own gentle pace she impaled the vulnerable core of her body on to his rigid prick. She sighed as she felt its length move up inside her. Peter lay very still. She was sure he had enough movement to be able to thrust his hips up to meet her. Perhaps he felt beaten and really subservient at last.

They'd made love like this before, with her on top. But Peter had always had his hands free. Now he couldn't fondle her. His forearms tensed as if out of habit, aching to feel her breasts.

'You can't reach,' Trudi chuckled from behind. 'But I can. Watch.'

She reached around Lia and cupped both her breasts. As Lia slowly began to move her hips up and down, Trudi fanned out her long fingers, caressing and then homing in to pinch her erect nipples tight. Lia rolled and thrust her hips just the way she wanted to. She was high and away from Peter's body but Trudi was giving her just the stimulation she needed. There was no hurry. Caught between two lovers she took precisely what pleasure she wanted from Peter's enslaved body.

The feel of the dildo inside her had been one thing. Sure enough, it had stretched her. It had been a delicious, unflagging fantasy experience. But there was nothing like the feel of a real, live, pulsing cock – flesh against flesh. She revelled in the sensation of Peter's erection moving within her, yet all the time she was in control, setting the pace, angling his penetration towards the vital spot inside.

There was a glow spreading out from her sex, warming the centre of her body and beyond, tingling up through her breasts as Trudi fondled them. She felt whole. She felt utterly womanly, beautiful and strong. Part of her wanted this feeling to carry on for ever.

But there was a build-up of impatience, too. The sweet but frustrating moment when she couldn't decide whether to spin out her pleasure longer or thrust just that little bit faster and let her orgasm come. Her patience gave out. She ground her body hard down on Peter's and the intensity triggered a climax so clasping it almost hurt as it swept through her lower body.

Peter was still hard inside her. For a split second she thought about swapping places with Trudi – but what if Peter was on the very brink? Besides, the feel of his cock inside her was still heaven, even after she'd come. She continued to thrust, relishing the hot, wet slipperiness of his maleness within her. He was very hard, now. He must be on the edge.

She felt him explode. He didn't cry out that loudly – perhaps with two women watching he felt more inhibited than usual. But the swell and kick inside her was indisputable. She loved to feel him come.

She waited till he'd gone soft again. Then she leaned forwards and kissed him – probably for the last time ever. 'Have we exhausted you?'

Peter grunted and nodded. That was all she needed to know.

They both lay down beside him. Lia played with his chest hair softly for a while. Trudi reached for the keys on the side and began unlocking his wrist and ankle restraints. Peter grunted again – presumably in approval – but otherwise didn't react.

Slowly the rhythm of his breathing changed. Lia felt a tug inside her chest: she knew that rhythm so well and what it meant. Did it mean she knew him? It didn't necessarily follow – or so she told herself.

'Well?' Trudi mouthed. Lia nodded.

They eased themselves carefully off the bed and stuffed everything in the rucksack. Lia hunted for her own clothes. Trudi looked down at her body suit and a little line appeared in the middle of her eyebrows as she wondered what to do about it.

'Keep it as a souvenir,' Lia whispered. 'I love you in it.'

Once dressed they crept downstairs. In Peter's office the light was still on and the door was ajar. When they pushed it fully open, Jules was sitting with her feet up at the desk, balancing the cup of coffee she'd helped herself to.

'Thought you two were never going to make an appearance.' She drained the cup. 'This is my sixth, I'll have you know, just to keep awake waiting for you.'

'But what happened?' Trudi demanded.

Jules grinned. 'Okay. I can see you're practically

imploding with the need to know.' She swung her feet off the desk. 'Massive VAT fraud. I knew there'd be something like that. No one like Peter Holme-Lacey is squeaky clean. But hey, this was mega. I e-mailed the VAT office from here – using his e-mail account. By lunchtime tomorrow I reckon they'll be crawling all over this place and he'll have to offload some of his non-essential assets pretty sharpish to pay the penalties. Hopefully the *Lady Jayne* will be high on his list.'

She scratched the back of her head and added ruefully, 'While you two were taking so long I did think of designing him a dinky little bouncing screensaver saying, "Believe it or not, this isn't the first time I've screwed a man. But it's been the most satisfying."'

'You didn't!'

'Don't panic. I know we don't want to make it *that* obvious we dumped him in it.' She picked up a couple of disks from the desk and waggled them. 'This is our web site stuff. It gets light around six so we can grab a few hours' kip before making a break for Jonathan's. We've got contacts to re-establish and a business to put back on track! And don't look like that, Lia. Anyone who can't think of something more inspired than "password" for his security password deserves to get shafted.'

CHAPTER

11

Lia opened one eye. The voices and electronic bleeps in the next room had woken her. She rolled over and squinted at Jonathan's alarm clock. Jules and Trudi were making an early start.

She turned lazily to the other side and looked at Jonathan. He was beautiful when he was asleep. Not in the same way as Denny. There was something feminine about the fine line of his jaw even through the dark stubble; he could only be bothered to shave every second or third day. He wasn't the standard macho man. He might not make every woman go weak at the knees. But there were things about him only she knew. Places in each other's heads only they had been together. No one else wrenched that tenderness from her. He got further through her defences than any other lover.

She reached over and stroked a soft line from one of his purple highlights to his temple to his cheek bone. She hadn't meant to wake him. She knew Jonathan didn't do mornings. But his eyes flickered open.

'Wha's time?'

'Nearly eight.'

'You're insatiable.'

'Hey – I didn't mean . . .'

He'd woken up amazingly quickly and rolled on top of her. Jonathan rarely dominated her physically and the novelty of it was spicy. Lia began to feel a stir of interest warming between her legs. All the more so when his semi-erect penis brushed against her inner thighs.

Beneath them the slats of Jonathan's futon creaked. They both grinned. Since they'd pulled their sting on Peter Holme-Lacey the past two weeks had been hectic for the girls. The last gasp of the summer holidays was in full swing and catering opportunities were there for the picking, but they'd spent as many nights here as they could manage, revamping the web site and getting their business contacts back in order. And Jonathan's bed had taken a bit of punishment.

'Didn't mean what?' he challenged.

'Nothing.'

Right now she was hardly about to protest. His erection had risen rapidly and the top of his shaft was pressing insistently against her sex. The warmth of his flesh excited her, the awareness that his blood was pumping madly, filling up his cock – and all for her. If he just eased his hips back a little, lowered them, then forwards . . . She parted her thighs, ready to give him a soft, moist welcome.

But Jonathan rolled off her body as suddenly as he'd rolled on. 'I've got another idea. Something I read about on a web site the other night. Was a new one on me.'

He slipped out of bed and padded over to a tall cupboard where he kept pretty much everything. Frustrated by the buzz between her thighs, Lia sat up and watched him rummage. She loved to see him naked. Right now his smooth, pale back was hunched over. She could just imagine running her hands down his bony spine. And as for that tiny, pert bum. Her palms literally itched to give it a squeeze.

Jonathan straightened up and turned. His cock was still high and she couldn't resist staring so she didn't realise for a second or two what he was holding.

'Crème de menthe?' She frowned. 'That's the kind of thing Auntie Faye would drink if she was really letting her hair down. Anyway, isn't it a little early in the day?'

'Just a few sips. It's the mint, apparently. Makes everything tingle. Let's give it a go.'

'I don't understand . . .'

'You will.' He grinned. She knew that wicked sparkle. 'In that case it's your turn first. Lie back. Relax . . .'

Jonathan whipped the duvet aside and snuggled himself down between her legs. She spread them a little wider. He took a small sip of the thick green liquid and snaked his tongue into her groove.

For a second or two nothing out of the ordinary seemed to be happening. Then Lia gasped. 'Tingle' was an understatement. Her sex was shiveringly cool and fiery all at the same time. It was the same sort of 'Wow!' factor your mouth gets when you brush with a new brand of toothpaste. Only, your mouth can't get randy as well . . .

Jonathan lifted his head and took another sip before wriggling his tongue as far as it would go between her pussy lips. She hadn't realised the tingling had begun to wear off. But when he tongued her again the chilling fire was even more intense. Her sex had never been so sensitive. She'd never felt every twitch of his tongue inside her so completely before.

Even when the initial violence of the chilling, fiery waves had died down there was a background buzz in her labia unlike anything she'd felt before. Oral sex always concentrated her whole awareness on her pussy – she didn't even need her nipples toyed with – but this was something else. The sheer unfamiliarity of it excited her; she couldn't remember being so thrilled since that long-ago night she'd stroked and rubbed herself to orgasm for the very first time.

Jonathan tipped the neck of the bottle on to her bush. Perhaps his hand slipped, perhaps he poured out a little more than he meant to, but a cold stream of fire trickled down over her clit and between her labia. It was more intense this time. Almost more than she could bear. His tongue was frantic, licking up all traces of crème de menthe. That oral frenzy brought her to the brink. Her orgasm expanded upwards into her body. The stretching, near-painful fullness of it was something special. Something only Jonathan had given her.

He rolled aside, grinning, and very carefully passed her the open bottle.

Lia took it and wriggled down the bed till her face was level with his cock, which was still meaty with interest. She blew slowly up and down the length of his shaft. He loved that. Jonathan gave a little throaty sound halfway between a chuckle and a moan. His cock began to twitch back into action.

Lia took a mouthful of the crème de menthe and swirled it round. Her gums began to tingle – the same hot-cold sensitivity she'd felt in her quim but subtler this time. More sensual than sexy. Her mouth felt totally alive. A tiny swig more, just to refresh the feeling, then she took Jonathan's plumped-up cock between her lips.

He took a sharp breath as she did so. The fiery sensation must be new to him, too. Sucking Jonathan was always a mutual pleasure but this time her pleasure was heightened as her own tongue danced with awareness, feeling the texture of his cock as never before.

There was only one drawback to this. The need to pause every few minutes to take another mouthful and renew the effects. From the almost audible rush of blood in his cock Lia realised she was bringing Jonathan right to the point of ejaculation and then leaving him hanging there as she paused to take a sip. She was torturing him. But Jonathan enjoyed a bit of torture.

'Wait,' she said just before taking yet another mouthful. 'I'm going to make this perfect for you.'

Tucked beneath his futon, she knew there was a tiny vibrator – barely thicker than her forefinger. She drew this out and dribbled some of the crème de menthe along it. Then she set it humming and slipped it into his anus. He gasped as the mintiness took effect.

She took his cock deep into her mouth again. She knew him so well – so intimately – she knew how the little vibrator was buzzing against the secret trigger spot deep inside him. It wouldn't be long now.

Jonathan's whole body stiffened and twisted on the bed. He cried out loud as he climaxed in her mouth, and as she felt his semen spurt into her it set those tingling sensations off again.

Lia waited a moment then drew the vibrator tenderly out of him. She hauled herself up his body and they kissed, deeply. Their lips were soft and slightly puffy from pleasuring each other's sex and their whole mouths still alive with that residual tingling. It felt the most complete, sharing kiss she'd ever had with a man.

'I can't believe you've never tried the "crème de menthe blow job" thing,' he said afterwards, 'given all the time you've been with a publican.'

'Denny's nowhere near as weird as you.'

'I know. That's why you love me.'

Damn. Why did he keep saying it and why could she never work out what to say back? Lia snuggled against Jonathan's soft-haired chest to avoid meeting his eyes. She became aware of the computer noises in the next room again.

'Jules and Trudi are more conscientious than you,' Jonathan murmured, giving her a playful slap on the buttock. 'Working instead of lazing in bed with their lovers.'

She giggled. Even just a few mouthfuls of liqueur on an empty stomach had gone to her head. 'Maybe they don't have that option. Is Jules pissed off with Lynne, still?'

'Don't your best mates tell you anything?'

'But that business with Marlene going off on Lynne's motorbike that night?'

He chuckled and dug her in the ribs. 'Well, I know something you don't. They came back here and compared and contrasted uniforms. That's all. Lynne's in love with Jules. It's sweet.'

Lia was about to bite back when Jonathan's intercom buzzed. She jumped.

'It'll just be the postman,' he murmured. 'Relax. And there's plenty left in that bottle. Wonder if the effect's the same if you drizzle it over your nipples . . .'

There was a loud knock on the bedroom door and after a brief pause Trudi opened it and stuck her head round. Lia was surprised she even bothered to knock.

'Li, it would be such a good idea if you got up and got your *covered* arse out here quick. Denny's on his way up.'

'Speak of the devil,' Jonathan grunted.

Lia rolled out of bed, sprang back up off the floor and grabbed a long T-shirt. It came down to about mid-thigh on her. It would have to do. She perched on the desk beside Jules and tried to look as though she'd been studying a computer screen all along.

Denny came in through the front door, a sheaf of mismatched envelopes in one hand. He ran the other through his tousled hair as he looked down at Lia. She knew it was a habit – a sign he wasn't quite sure of his ground.

'You said any post that came might be urgent,' he said, handing over the sheaf. 'Or at least your *text* did. So I thought I'd better drop this round.'

His barb left her at a loss for words. She'd deserved that. Yes, the past couple of weeks had been frantic, but Denny was only five miles away and she could have made time to see him. Instead she'd taken the cowardly option of texting him a few brief messages.

'We've been busy,' she mumbled, and couldn't think of anything else to say with Jules's and Trudi's eyes on her.

Then she was aware that Denny wasn't focusing on her. She looked over her shoulder and realised Jonathan had got up, thrown on his Chinese-style dressing gown and was standing in the open bedroom door.

'Clearly,' Denny replied frostily. 'I've got a supplier to see in town. I'd better dash if I'm to get back for lunchtime opening.'

After Denny had closed the door behind him, Trudi gave a slow hand clap. 'Brilliant timing, Jonathan. Now you're up, go make yourself useful. Mine's black, one sugar in case you've forgotten.'

Lia sorted the post into an 'interesting' and 'boring' pile. There was a white, typed envelope with a smudged postmark she couldn't quite make out. She didn't even wait long enough to put it on the 'interesting' pile.

'Hey guys, Auntie Faye's got herself a word processor at last! Oh . . . she wants to meet up with us this Sunday. That rather posh new tea shop opposite the fountain. She says she's looked at our web site and worked out it's one of the few days we don't have any bookings in the next week or so. Auntie Faye getting wired! I can't believe it.'

'Never mind about that,' Trudi snapped, looking over her shoulder. 'If she wants to meet up so urgently it must be because she's thinking of buying back the *Lady Jayne*.' Her hand reached across the mouse mat and tightened on Jules's.

'Holme-Lacey must have been in touch with her. He must realise she's the only person who'd buy the old girl at short notice. We'll have him off our backs!'

'I hope so.' Lia passed the letter round. 'But let's not celebrate just yet. We haven't heard a word from him. He may be plotting something.'

'This Sunday?' Jules re-read the letter, frowning.

'Is there a problem?'

'Lynne's asked me to Sunday lunch with her folks.'

'But this is important.'

'So's meeting Lynne's folks. This is the first time anyone's asked me back to meet her parents. As me. As her partner. Not just pretending to be good friends.'

Trudi looked uneasy. 'You know I'd have introduced you properly to Mom and Dad. But Jo'burg's a bit further than North Oxfordshire.'

'All the same, you see why this matters to me. And like you say, Lia, it's the only free Sunday we've got coming up. And the last time I got in a meeting with you two over the boat's future it didn't exactly go well. I don't mind if you do this one without me.'

Lia made her way across the cobbled, pedestrianised street. It was that kind of bright September day with a foreboding of chill in the air but it didn't seem to put off any tourists who were still buying ice-creams by the dozen and watching street entertainers near the fountain. That was what she loved about Stratford. It didn't have a tourist season as such. Something was always going on.

Auntie Faye had good news for them. Lia could just feel it – despite warning the others to rein in their hopes. And just yesterday they'd had a call from Jules's brief employers, Vegetable Love, who were doing so well they wanted to talk about linking up over the winter. It would give them the breathing space they needed. If Trudi didn't wind them up by mentioning rare fillet steak every five minutes . . .

Lia was so absorbed in plans for the next few months she lost track of where she was going and walked into the bonnet of a Morgan sports car parked on a double yellow. The man in the driver's seat looked up sharply. Lia mouthed 'Sorry' and ducked quickly into the tea shop.

'You're late,' Trudi hissed from a window table. 'She's in the Ladies. And she's *your* godmother – I never know what to say to her that won't land us all in trouble. Where did you get to?'

Lia eased herself gingerly into a free chair and snatched the napkin before the hovering waitress could put it on her lap. She'd rather do that herself at the moment.

'Something to do on the way. Took longer than I reckoned on. Ah, here she comes. Tell you later.'

Faye had changed her hairstyle to a neat, grey bob, Lia saw as her godmother walked briskly across the room. And her clothes were more vivid. They made her look younger. Then Lia realised she'd never been sure how old Faye Montgomery was.

'Cream teas all round,' Faye told the waitress. 'Actually, make that four.' As the girl walked away, Lia caught Trudi gazing after her. Yes, that black skirt was tight across an unreasonably pert young bum. But they had to concentrate. Lia kicked Trudi under the table. Trudi smirked back. She thinks I'm jealous! Lia realised. Of course I'm not . . .

'Girls,' Faye continued, apparently oblivious to scufflings around the table legs, 'things have changed. It seems Peter Holme-Lacey has cash-flow problems himself. Did you have any inkling of it?'

Lia bit down on the insides of her cheeks. It was the only way she could keep a straight face.

'He phoned me the week before last,' Faye went on. 'Phoned me himself, didn't even get his secretary to do it. Offered to sell me back the *Lady Jayne* at quite a bit less than I paid for it. I said I needed time to think and he got quite jumpy. Ah, here's our tea.'

The waitress placed a cream tea in the empty fourth place, too. Trudi and Lia shrugged at one another but didn't say anything. It was usually best to humour Faye.

'You should take him up on it,' Trudi said quickly, through a mouthful of scone. 'Before he changes his mind.'

Faye put her silver knife down delicately. 'Ah, there's a problem. My own finances aren't suffi-ciently recovered. But let me tell you a little story.'

Lia rolled her eyes. She'd heard many of Faye's 'little stories' when she was growing up. They usually had a tedious moral point.

'I've been getting friendly with the young man whose family live next door.'

That figured, Lia thought. Auntie Faye collected protégés like other women her age collected stray cats.

'He's been teaching me about the Internet. I

believe they call it 'silver surfing' at my age. I went and looked at your web site. It's rather good. I tried to send you some e-mails but I don't suppose you ever got them.'

'That would probably be around the time Holme-Lacey was scuppering the whole thing,' Trudi muttered but Lia kicked her ankle again. The less Faye knew, the better.

'Anyway, I started clicking on – what do you call those things that trundle across the top of the page?'

'Banner ads, Auntie.'

'Yes, them. Just to see what would happen. Next thing I know I'm exchanging e-mails with this gentleman who . . .' She paused. Lia looked up. Was Auntie Faye really blushing? 'He's rather *different*. But that's not important. What is important is that he's an entrepreneur. Looking to make investments. After Mr Holme-Lacey's proposal, I contacted him to see if he'd be interested in buying back the *Lady Jayne* with me, jointly. Of course, I wanted to ask you girls your opinion first this time. After the last fiasco.'

Lia narrowed her eyes at her godmother – who didn't seem to be quite as naïve as she'd thought.

'And you know him,' Faye continued, 'or at least know of him. Neil Harper. His nephew is your young friend who's such a whiz with computers.'

Jonathan's uncle – the property developer. It was all falling into place. Lia's thoughts were reeling. And if he was content to leave Jonathan in peace to manage the block of flats, surely he'd be similarly hands-off with them? It could be the perfect solution. She looked across the table at

Trudi who was nodding as if the same idea was going through her head.

'Turn round and wave at him then, dear,' Faye said. 'He's in the sports car just across the street and his tea will be going cold. I'd text him like you girls do, but I still haven't got the hang of those mobile things.'

Over her shoulder Lia watched a man get out of the sports car she'd walked into. Oops. Not the most sophisticated first impression. He walked up to them casually – the same body movements, the same grace she knew in Jonathan. His hair was loose, iron-grey curls but there was something familiar about the eyes, too. Jonathan's maverick, impish look.

When he sat down in the fourth chair something girlish happened to Auntie Faye's face. Lia shrugged. She really didn't want to imagine it.

'Listen,' Trudi said after formalities and pleasantries were out of the way. 'We're cool about the situation. You guys go ahead and do whatever you have to do with solicitors and stuff, and let us know when there's something we need to look over. Just don't try to run things for us. That's our game.'

'As if I'd dream of it. And I believe you have to go and set up for some historical re-enactment tomorrow near Henley-in-Arden. Or so your web site says. Don't let me keep you.' He offered his hand before they left. He held Lia's firmly and for a long time before he let go. She met his eyes – Jonathan's eyes. Here was a middle-aged guy who still had that definite spark. This time, her instinct told her, things were going to work.

She and Trudi linked arms as they walked out

into the mellow September sunshine. It had warmed up since they'd been inside. Trudi let her breath out in a long sigh. 'Life. Full of surprises, eh?'

'Yeah,' Lia agreed. 'And right now I don't want to think about it, I just want to get on with mine.'

'Surprises?'

'Life.'

'You were mad at me for eyeing up that waitress's cute arse.'

'Behave.' Lia dug Trudi in the ribs.

'Okay. Going to tell me why you were late?'

'You'll see. I—' Lia froze. They were in sight of the *Lady Jayne*'s mooring. 'Trudi! There's a policewoman coming out of the barge. She's leading Jules away. She's handcuffed her!'

Lia broke away and began running down the riverside path. She was an idiot to think it could have been that easy. Peter had been biding his time. Somewhere along the line they must have done something illegal. He'd set the police on to them. The future she'd been planning only that morning was viciously snatched away. There was a tightness burning in her throat and all she could do now was try to help her friend.

Behind her she heard Trudi calling, 'Wait – no!' but Lia was already level with Jules and grabbed her by the shoulder.

Lynne and Jules turned round, bemused. They were still holding hands. No cuffs.

'Eh? What?' Lia stammered. 'Someone mind telling me . . . Weren't you a traffic warden?'

By this time Trudi had jogged up behind her. The rest of them swapped sheepish grins which made Lia fume. She felt left out of the loop again.

'I thought you realised,' Lynne said, smoothing down her police woman's uniform self-consciously. 'I'm a speciality strippergram. Just had a short-notice lunchtime job at the cricket club – someone's leaving do. Don't worry.' She winked. 'We'll nip back to the flat and I'll change before showing up at my mum's.'

A lesbian strippergram? Lia mused, too busy suppressing giggles to be mad any more. Now I really have heard everything!

'So that would explain the wigs you lent us that time?'

'I thought you two were supposed to be gone by now?' Trudi said.

'Yeah – well . . .' Jules looked at Lynne tenderly. 'We kind of got delayed.' Then she did her best to suppress her smirk and looked directly at Lia and Trudi. 'What happened with Faye?'

'Oh.' The last few minutes' had nearly driven the meeting from Lia's mind. 'Looks like Jonathan's uncle could be our new part-owner.'

Jules nodded thoughtfully. 'That could work. I met him a few times when I was crashing at Jonathan's while you two . . . Anyway, I'll catch up with you first thing tomorrow at Henley. Lynne'll give me a lift on the bike. Take care, guys.'

They walked off again, hand in hand. Lia shook her head and climbed aboard the *Lady Jayne*. 'I don't think I could take any more surprises today,' she said as she started the engine.'

'Wasn't planning on springing any on you,' Trudi replied.

The sun grew even warmer as they took the canal upstream. Trudi stripped down to a scanty bikini and lay on the top deck reading – or pretending to read – a book while Lia steered. It was difficult to concentrate on keeping the tiller steady. Trudi was facing her and propped up on her elbows in such a way that her warm breasts hung close together and seemed to be slowly slipping forwards in their bikini cups. Lia just had to stare. And then she realised Trudi hadn't turned over a page in quite some time.

'Li, be a mate and rub some sunblock into my back?'

'Like you need it with your skin.'

'Can't be too careful.'

Trudi swung down from the top deck, disappeared inside the barge and came back a few minutes later with some factor 30 – presumably belonging to fair-skinned Jules. She sat beside Lia at the tiller and turned her back to her.

'You're not making this easy for me,' Lia muttered as she steered one-handed, the other hand smoothing the thick cream across Trudi's shoulders.

Trudi was such a pleasure to touch. Her skin seemed to absorb the sun's warmth and then let it out lazily when stroked. And there was real muscle beneath that skin. Sexy muscle. Lia's fingers glided over her shoulder blades and the sensuous curve of her deltoids. Her hands did their own dance on Trudi's skin. She didn't have to think about it. Long after the sunblock had been absorbed she carried on following instinct with her caress.

She moved forwards to stroke Trudi's collar bones. It was so tempting to carry on down and feel her breasts. Her fingers began to stretch forwards, exploring . . .

A barge coming the other way blasted its horn.

Lia snatched the tiller back quickly. Her heart was pounding with what might have been.

'We don't want another accident,' Trudi murmured.

'You're driving me crazy. And you know it.'

'Moor up, then. Are we in such a rush?'

In the dim, peaceful cabin there was very little left of Trudi's clothes to peel off. Lia let her hands roam free, gliding down the extravagant upper curves of those tawny breasts, circling that taut, muscular waist. Trudi tugged at the side zip of Lia's skirt as Lia sank down on to the narrow bunk. As the skirt fell away a chink of sunlight through the almost-closed curtains glinted on the simple titanium ring in Lia's belly button.

Trudi grinned and drew a wide circle around it with her forefinger. 'So that's what made you late. We can have a lot of fun with that – when it's properly healed. In the meantime . . .' She dropped on to the bed beside Lia and began kissing her way over her lower belly. 'We'll just have to start a bit lower down.'